Praise for Lexxie Couper's
The Sun Sword

"If you want a romance that keeps you one the edge, makes you cry and sigh, and takes you to new worlds, I highly recommend *The Sun Sword.*"

~ *Whipped Cream Reviews*

"The plot's twists and turns really held my attention, and the main characters, particularly Torrin, tugged at my heart. Torrin is stalwart, proud and honorable. Kala is vulnerable, but stubborn and obviously used to doing things her way. And as for Ms. Couper's truly nasty villain, I wanted to kill the remorseless blackguard myself!"

~ *Fallen Angel Reviews*

"Ms. Couper has given us a very exciting and enticing story with many twist and turns that make this book a great read."

~ *The Romance Studio*

Look for these titles by *Lexxie Couper*

Now Available:

Savage Retribution
Savage Transformation
Death, the Vamp and his Brother

The Sun Sword

Lexxie Couper

A Samhain Publishing, Ltd. publication.

Samhain Publishing, Ltd.
577 Mulberry Street, Suite 1520
Macon, GA 31201
www.samhainpublishing.com

The Sun Sword
Copyright © 2010 by Lexxie Couper
Print ISBN: 978-1-60504-822-2
Digital ISBN: 978-1-60504-832-1

Editing by Heidi Moore
Cover by Kanaxa

First Samhain Publishing, Ltd. electronic publication: November 2009
First Samhain Publishing, Ltd. print publication: October 2010

Dedication

For Dags. Who made me watch *Dr Who* when I should have been watching *Sesame Street*. Love you, Bro.

To Jessica Russell. Thank you for letting me chase the sun with you. You are, as I've always said, gorgeous.

The old gods, the Immortals, looked at what the worlds of man had become and wept. Their tears extinguished the burning hearts of the universes and for eons there was only cold. Darkness.

Millennia passed. The Immortals watched the worlds of man turn heartless and violent. Their grief turned to rage and their rage turned to resolve.

The Eldest reached into the very heart of existence and forged a blade from its simmering core. A blade of infinite light and never-ending dark. A blade to end life and begin it.

The Youngest saw the fates of the worlds of man and stole the blade, hiding it in the twin souls of life. The Youngest then placed a seed in time and the seed would be the true wielder. When the worlds of man balanced on the cusp of self-destruction, the lone warrior would find the hope and the hope would be the One Who Burns and the One Who Burns would be the end and the beginning.

The Eldest saw the seed and, furious at its possibility, perverted its form. The One Who Burns would not be alone. There would be another, one who burned just as fiercely. A fire of infinite rage. The False Fire.

And the worlds of man would suffer.

Or rejoice.

The *Sol* Edict, Book One. Author unknown.

The One Who Burns will walk the grounds of despair, soul empty of peace, heart ripe with hate.

The False Fire will walk the grounds of despair, soul empty of peace, heart ripe with hate.

Both shall be destroyed. Both shall be victorious. Both will bring death and darkness when the lone heart bleeds and the stone weeps.

The *Sol* Prophecy. Book Fourteen. The Oracle.

"The Oracle told us the Sun Sword will bring new life to the hearts of man in the hands of the One Who Burns.

The Oracle also told us the Sun Sword will bring brutal death to the hearts of man in the hands of the False Fire.

What the Oracle failed to tell us, the irritating old crone, was how to tell whom was whom."

An Account of the Failure of the Oracle. Cai of P'helios

Prologue

Earth calendar 2445

Torin Kerridon walked down the rubbish-strewn street, studying the derelict buildings, stunted fauna and polluted sky. *So, this is Earth.*

He curled his nose, moving his right hand closer to his disruptor. He didn't expect anyone to attack him—he doubted anyone still living on the once-prosperous planet was healthy enough to pose any threat—but that didn't mean he relaxed his guard.

You relaxed your guard, you died. That was the way of the *Sol.*

Besides, somewhere on this forgotten hunk of dying rock was a warrior of supreme force and skill. A warrior more deadly than the entire *Sol* Order combined. Even if he didn't know it yet.

Stepping over a fallen tree, the leaves long dead, the branches withered and twisted as though tortured, Torin scanned the immediate area. The Old Seer had sworn the One Who Burns could be found somewhere in this vicinity. He'd been quite adamant about it in fact, almost having an apoplexy when Torin had voiced his doubt.

The old man had refused to listen to reason and, invoking the *Sol* Edict, had commanded Torin leave P'helios immediately for the abandoned planet.

Casting a dubious look at the closest building, boarded-up windows doing little to hide its desolate decay, Torin shook his head. The Old Seer was never wrong. If he said the One Who Burns was here, he was here. Somewhere. The southern hemisphere of the planet had survived the Third Global with the least destruction, the planet's ailing weather patterns saving it from the initial bio detonation. Torin looked up at the sky and scowled. Polluted storm clouds boiled and rolled above him. The Old Seer had drawn the constellation under which Torin would find the One Who Burns, sightless eyes staring at the parchment as he'd inked the angled five-starred cross. The map however was useless.

Returning his attention to the buildings around him, Torin continued forward. He didn't need to see the stars to know he was in the correct location. The sensors on his ship, *Helios Blade*, indicated a significant number of life signs in this quadrant. The only sign of life on the eastern coastline of the large landmass to be exact—a paltry four hundred and forty-two souls. According to the Old Seer, the One Who Burns was among them.

Torin frowned, looking at the empty, desolate dwellings around him. *How are you going to find him, Kerridon?*

He let out a silent grunt, his skepticism pushed further by his bleak surrounds. The Old Seer had told him the One Who Burns would find him, but he couldn't help wondering how.

"The One will come to you. Walk through the streets of dismay with want in your soul, belief in your heart and the One will come to you. This you must do. Or the hearts of man will be—"

His proclamation had ended there. The Old Seer's sightless eyes had rolled back into his ancient head, he'd hitched in a sharp breath and died.

Torin clenched his fist, the memory of his *Sol* guide's death still jarring. The Old Seer had charged him with a task and he must obey. He was the last of the *Sol* Order. The last warrior charged with the protection of the Sun Sword, the ultimate weapon in the known universes. A weapon forged by the Immortals and discovered by the Oracle. A weapon created to end all life and begin it. He needed to find the one who was born to wield the blade before the False Fire did. If he failed, the worlds of man would cease to—

A ball of solid steel smashed into his chest, hurling him backward. His heels tripped, his feet tangled and, before he knew it, he was on his back staring at the bruised, polluted sky. Pain radiated through him. *Syunna, what was that?*

He flipped his body from the filth-strewn ground, disruptor drawn.

And found a tiny slip of a girl no taller than his chest standing before him, green eyes burning with golden fire, short black hair a spiky crown of mess. She glared at him, a long, rusted steel pipe clenched in her small fists. "Whoever you are, you're not welcome here," she growled, her voice husky. And angry. Very angry.

Torin frowned, resisting the urge to lift his hand and rub his chest. By the gods, what had she hit him with?

What do you mean, she? Surely you don't think this whelp put you on your arse, do you?

He returned his disruptor to its holster. "I have no issue with you, girl." He began walking forward. "Move aside before I put you across my knee and—"

She threw herself at him. Feet first.

Her bootless heels struck his gut like two small balls of steel. He stumbled again, dumbstruck.

She swung the pipe, smashing it against his jaw as he fell.

White agony detonated in his head. He let out a shout of rage and indignation. How could a scrap of a child move so quickly? And hit so hard?

Before he could contemplate the answer, she straddled his chest, the steel pipe rammed under his chin. Choking him.

She glared down at him, the fury in her eyes seismic. "I will not let your *kind* touch me again."

Torin stared at her, teeth clenched. "I'm not going to touch you. Now get off me before I give you a damn good—"

She didn't let him finish. Fear flooded her eyes, turning the rage there to icy terror. She smashed the pipe against his face, his jaw, his shoulders, her tiny body trembling, her face set.

Pain erupted in his head. He let out a shout, more of surprise than agony, and grabbed at her wrists.

She was quick.

He was quicker.

Before she could strike him again with that cursed steel pipe, he yanked her body forward, threw her to ground beside him and rolled on top of her, pinning her beneath his weight.

"Get off me!" she screamed, thrashing and bucking like a wild animal.

He dodged another attempted blow from her right hand, fighting to keep her wrists in his grip.

Syunna, she's strong for a scrap.

"Get off, me get off me, *get off me!*"

Her scream grew louder with every word, her eyes wider and more terrified.

"Stop it!" he roared, smacking her wrists to the ground beside her head and staring down into her muck-smeared face.

"I'm not going to hurt you."

"Ha!" she barked. "I've heard that before. Right before one of your kind shoves his dick between my legs."

Cold fury rolled through Torin. His gut clenched at the implication behind her words and he fixed her with a steady look. "I, Torin Kerridon, last command warrior of the *Sol* Order and keeper of the Sun Sword's truth, swear I will never bring harm upon your body." He relaxed his hold on her wrists. A little. "Nor shove my dick between your legs."

She glared up at him, green eyes flashing golden chips of rage.

He loosened his hold a fraction more. "This is my word and I swear it to you on my honour."

She stopped fighting against his weight, expression guarded. Wary. "I swear I will rip your dick off and shove it down your throat if you break your word."

The words were full of promise and Torin didn't doubt—if given the chance—she would be capable of doing just so. He frowned, his gut still tight. "What is your name, child?"

Her jaw bunched, defiant strength glinting in her unusual eyes, and she shifted beneath him. "I'm not a child. I'm almost twenty-one."

Torin suppressed the urge to smile. Almost twenty-one made her a child by his reasoning, and by his own advanced age. "What is your name, *child?*" he repeated, the need to know growing heavy in his gut.

Green eyes glinted. "Kala Rei. Now get off me."

But Torin couldn't move. He stared down at the dirty, skinny girl, every muscle in his body locked frozen with disbelief, his heart a thumping beat, his blood roaring in his ears.

Kala Rei.

The name whispered by the Immortals. The name he'd known all his life.

Kala Rei.

The One Who Burns.

Chapter One

Six Earth months later

Kala opened her eyes and gazed up at the low, metal ceiling. It hung above her head as it had for the last six months, a solid plane of dull grey that reflected no light and radiated no life. Closing her eyes again, she stayed stretched on her hard, narrow bunk and began a slow count of one hundred. With each number, she flexed and coiled the muscles in her body, the process beginning with her toes and ending with her fingers.

Heat flowed through her, the meditation routine waking her body, preparing her for what was to come.

What? Another day spent covered in sweat and blood? Your body aching, your muscles bruised? The bloody great big sword he makes you sleep with tearing your shoulders from their joints every time you swing it? This has to stop, Kala. The man is as crazy as a cut snake.

Opening her eyes again, she stared at her quarter's ceiling and saw the God-cursed bastard who'd taken her from hell.

He was never far from her thoughts, Torin Kerridon. Not a minute passed during the hours she was awake when she didn't think of him—curse him, wish he were dead. Pictured the massive sword he'd thrust into her hands the second she'd boarded his ship plunging into his hard, flat gut. Pictured the life fading from his storm-grey eyes.

Not a minute passed during the brief hours she slept when she didn't dream of him—of his hands skimming her naked legs, his mouth brushing over the small swells of her breasts, his lips closing over one nipple to suckle on its puckered tip as his fingers caressed the other.

A tight dampness knotted in the pit of her belly and she let out a sharp growl. She snapped upright on her bunk, swung her legs around and dropped to the floor, punching out an endless number of pushups in an effort to rid her mind of those tormenting nighttime images.

It was an exercise in futility. It always was. Every morning she went through the same routine. The realization, the meditation, the memories, the wanting. Every morning she punished herself for her weakness with an absurd amount of pushups.

And you think Torin is the crazy one? You desire a man you long to see dead.

Letting the strength evaporate from her arms, back and shoulders, Kala slumped to the floor. She pressed her flushed forehead against its icy metal surface. Nothing made sense anymore. Six months ago she was fighting to survive on a long forgotten planet, a lone female with no family or connections, forsaken as a child by a person whose face time had erased. A young girl forced to grow up by the harsh brutality of her existence, raped, assaulted and bashed repeatedly because of what was between her legs. A young girl praying for death to find her every night, fighting it with every molecule in her body when it came in the form of vile men with hard dicks and black souls. Six months ago, she knew the meaning of her existence—pain. Lots of pain. Now...

What would it be like? To be held by someone, loved by

someone who didn't want to hurt her? To be cherished and worshipped, not used and abused. Someone who touched her to bring *her* pleasure, not take it for himself?

Someone like Torin?

Flattening her palms against the chilly floor, she pushed herself to her feet and crossed the confining space of her quarters. A shower. She needed a shower. In exactly thirty minutes she would be covered in sweat again, the bastard *Sol* warrior pushing her body to its limits in that damn torture chamber he called a training room, but she needed to cleanse herself before the pain began.

A cold shower also afforded her the briefest moments of privacy. Torin Kerridon did not balk at walking into her quarters any time of the day or night—when he deemed training had begun, it began, regardless of the hour. When she stood inside her shower cubicle however, the cold water streaming over her flesh, through her tangle and dirt-free hair, over her lips and nipples, he respected her privacy.

And don't you wish he didn't. Don't you wish he would storm into your quarters, smash his fist against the shower's door control, wrap his fingers around your wrists and yank you from under the water, pulling you against his body and doing everything he could to make you feel—

Kala ground her teeth. "Stop it!"

She was just as insane as the man who'd taken her from Earth. He thought she was some long-prophesied warrior, destined to save the worlds of man from some unspeakable evil, and she thought he was—

Kala yanked the minimal clothing she wore to sleep from her body and stepped into the shower, shutting the thought down. It was lunacy. She didn't desire him. He was an insane man with delusions of grandeur from a planet she'd never heard of, let alone been to. She was only going along for the ride because what he offered was better than what she'd spent the first twenty-one years of her life living. The dreams and fantasies stemmed from the simple fact he'd saved her from that life. That was it. Nothing more.

Yeah, right. You keep telling yourself that, Kala.

Punching the hydro stream control, she lifted her face into the cold blast of water, eyes squeezed shut, fists clenched. "Shut the fuck up."

Two minutes later—skin like ice, centre like fire—she stepped from the tiny cubicle, dripping wet and still just as angry. She'd had enough. Today was the day she ended it. She'd let the insanity go on for too long.

It was time to tell Torin she wanted to—

"I am sorry. I did not intend—"

The hurried apology, spoken in a voice so deep it was almost a growl, made Kala jump and she spun about, her hands balling into fists instantly, her sex constricting just as fast.

Torin Kerridon stood in the entryway of her quarters, his massive frame almost filling it completely. His face appeared to be carved from stone, expressionless and unreadable, and his eyes studied the floor to the right of her feet. He shifted slightly and for a moment Kala wanted to burst out laughing. The man could probably kill an Earth grizzly with his bare hands and here he was looking nervous for finding her naked.

Make him more nervous, Kala. Make him sweat. Make him suffer.

The dark, unexpected thought whispered through her head and her nipples tightened, her pussy squeezing in a flutter of tight pulses. She locked her stare on his face, wanting those angry-sky eyes of his to turn her way. To look at her, see her.
20

Wanting them to fill with carnal desire and tormented confusion.

She wanted to shout, "Look at me!"

But she didn't.

She didn't have to.

Torin swung his head toward her, his face a granite mask, his eyes...

Kala lifted her chin, her pulse pounding. His eyes were turbulent. They drilled into hers, as if he could not look elsewhere.

Make him.

A tight shiver rippled through her and her lips parted with a soft gasp. She straightened her spine and pulled a deep breath, letting her breasts rise as she did so.

Look at me.

His stare didn't leave her face.

She touched the tip of her tongue to her bottom lip.

His nostrils flared.

Look at me. She took another breath, the pit of her stomach knotting. *All of me. Please.*

Torin's jaw bunched. His nostrils flared again and then he turned in the entryway, presenting her the sight of his broad back, the blazing sun tattooed across its muscled expanse hidden by the worn leather vest he wore. "Training will begin in ten." He threw the words over his shoulder in a blunt command. "Do not be late."

Kala nodded, despite the fact he did not look at her. Torin stood motionless in the entryway, the silence growing so thick she could barely draw breath. A long second passed. Followed by an even longer one.

She stared at him. Willed him to turn around.

His fists clenched, his shoulders bunched and then, with a muttered curse in a language she didn't understand, he strode away, disappearing from her sight.

Kala let out a choked sigh, closing her eyes and dropping her still-damp face into her still-damp hands. She had to get off this ship. She didn't believe in prophesies and destinies and saviors. She believed in pain. And she'd had enough of it. Both physical and—since the hulking man with the grey eyes and insane ideas came into her life—emotional. It was time to leave it all behind and get away.

Storming to her bunk, she snatched up her training attire—leather trousers two sizes too big for her and the snakeskin vest she'd been wearing when Torin "rescued" her from Earth. They were the only two items of clothing she could wear. Her trousers—the original pair she'd worn back on Earth had disintegrated the minute she'd tried to clean them once coming aboard *Helios Blade*, leaving her with nothing but the snakeskin vest and her pride. Torin had given her the leather trousers when she'd come to him, angry, embarrassed and wrapped in a towel from the hips down. Where he'd procured them, she didn't know. Despite their size, they would be too small for him. The quick look he'd given her in his own quarters, face expressionless, jaw clenched, spoke of displeasure and frustration.

Six months later, Kala knew he still harbored those same emotions. Whatever Torin Kerridon, last command warrior of the *Sol* Order and keeper of the Sun Sword's truth had expected to find on Earth, she knew she wasn't it.

A boy. He was expecting to find a boy. A male. The One Who bloody Burns, not some little girl. Someone strong and hard. Someone not you.

Grinding her teeth, the familiar thought scratching at her nerves, Kala snatched up the long, thick blade tangled in the sheets of her bunk. She lifted its tip level with her eyes. It was sharp. Wicked in its lethal edge. She'd spent every day since coming aboard Torin's ship with it in her hands. Learning how to use it, fight with it. Kill with it. It was ancient. A weapon from a lifetime ago.

It was also an imposter. *Not* the sword of which Torin believed her to be the destined wielder. *That* sword—the Sun Sword—she had yet to see, let alone hold.

"Not until you are ready."

The memory of his proclamation uttered to her the seventh day aboard his ship sent a ball of angry heat down into her belly. She swung the training sword down, the swoosh it made cutting the air like the sound of old ice shearing in two. Something in his eyes, something dark, something troubled, told Kala there was more to Torin's reticence than her current physical ability. Whatever it was however, the warrior refused to divulge and any time she pressed him—which she did almost every day—he increased the punishing intensity of her training.

With a sharp shake of her head and a low snort of disgust, she cast the small room one last look. It had been her home for half an Earth solar cycle, the longest she'd ever stayed in one place, the longest she'd ever felt safe, but enough was enough.

She tightened her grip on the heavy sword and walked through the doorway. It was time to go. Before she went just as insane as the *Sol* warrior.

Torin stood in the training room—an area in *Helios Blade*'s aft dedicated to the preparation of the One Who Burns, equipped with every weapon Kala needed to be proficient with, every weapon she needed to be an expert at defending against. His eyes were closed and he pulled deep, steady breaths of his ship's artificial air into his lungs through his nose, forcing the heat in his body to subside.

The shower. Syunna. He'd found her in the shower.

Well, technically, just *out* of the shower.

Curse it. Were the old gods taunting him for fun, tormenting him to see his suffering, or was there a purpose to their actions?

Unbidden, an image of the bane of his existence stepping from the shower cubicle flooded his head. Glistening beads of water trickled down her small lithe body, charting seductive paths over her breasts and belly and thighs and he wanted nothing more than to follow them with his tongue. Her drenched hair clung to her back and shoulders like black silk, highlighting the column of her neck, the straightness of her posture, her sinewy but still feminine muscles moving under her smooth brown skin with fluid strength.

A scalding knot of repressed hunger tightened in the pit of his belly, making his groin stir and his pulse quicken.

He bunched his fists, forcing the base response aside. That he harbored such carnal wants disgusted him. Filled him with contempt. Kala Rei was the last hope for the worlds of man against a future too horrific to ponder. She was not an object to desire. To lust after.

Oh, but you do desire her, Kerridon. You do lust after her. Every minute of every hour of every gods-cursed day.

He pulled in another deep breath, slower this time, directing the thrumming urgency in his body to subside. The last six months had been a long, drawn-out torture with no end in sight. Every time the One Who Burns drew close to him—her skin wet with perspiration, her chest heaving with exertion, her eyes blazing with hate and rage—his blood turned hot and his balls grew tight. Every time she crossed his path outside the training area—on her way to the galley or her quarters, her body uncharged with the wild energy of his preparation, her steps wary, her expression more so—he wanted to take her into his arms, hold her close to his heart and make her feel safe.

He retired to his quarters every night, exhausted from the sheer willpower it took to *not* throw her against the wall of his ship and take her every time he saw her, to *not* show her the rapture of true pleasure and the serenity of complete rapture. The training of the *Sol* warrior was the most brutal and grueling in the known universes but what he endured in the presence of the One Who Burns, the tiny slip of a female no taller than his chin, made that training look like a high-summer picnic.

He had but one hope and one hope only. Get her to the Sun Sword as soon as possible. Get her to the Immortals' weapon before the False Fire. See the weapon in her hand, its true and destined wielder, and then get as far from her as possible. Before he did what he swore to her six months ago on the dying surface of planet Earth he would *never* do. Stick his dick between her legs.

A low growl rumbled in the base of his throat and he dug his fingers into his palms. Time was his enemy, *their* enemy. All would be lost if he didn't find the Sun Sword soon.

All will be lost if you don't remove yourself from Kala Rei's presence soon.

Torin growled again. That was not possible. Until the sword was found, until the One Who Burns held it in her grasp, he could never leave her presence. It was too dangerous for the worlds of man. It was too dangerous for *her*.

And whenever her green eyes raze your form, Torin

Kerridon, it is too dangerous for you too.

"By the gods," he muttered, shaking his head, "if I could resurrect the Old Seer I would strangle him."

A soft scratching behind Torin made him tense. He sucked in a sharp breath, the air about him suddenly sweet and intoxicating. He caught his groan—part frustration, part carnal want, part self-loathing desperation—before it could rumble up his throat.

She had arrived. The One Who Burns. She stood but a few feet away, waiting for his very command.

Then command her to—

Opening his eyes, he studied the wall opposite. The training room's array of weapons adorned its metal span, all deadly in the right hands, all beyond deadly in his. It had only taken six months for Kala to be a master at each, no matter their origin in space or time. Just as the Old Seer had foretold.

He clenched his teeth, her prowess reigniting the heat in his groin. "You are thirty-five seconds late."

He could feel the hot hate in her glare.

"Yes."

The single word turned his already too-fast pulse to a rapid tattoo. He felt Kala shift on her feet, the air around him rippling with the slight movement, the noise like a loud hiss over the hum of his ship's propulsion engines. There was a low scraping sound, metal on leather, followed by the sound of her feet shifting again.

His mouth went dry and he curled his fingers into fists. "We do not train with the sword today."

Silence met his blunt statement. So absolute he could hear his own heart hammering. She was surprised. Thrown off-guard.

He swallowed, throat tight. "Today we train hand-to-hand combat."

Are you mad? You are going to touch her? Skin-to-skin, flesh-to-flesh? Do you really want to torture yourself more than you already are?

"Hand-to-hand?"

Her voice was steady, cut with that same confronting aggression he'd heard the very first time he saw her, blocking his path on Earth. But underneath the clipped syllables, a waver reverberated. A tremble so slight he almost missed it.

He scowled, the realization making his skin prickle. He spent hours convincing himself every day she was the ultimate warrior of destiny, and with just three words his tenuous conviction was shattered. She unnerved him. Unsettled him. Weakened him.

Dangerous, Torin Kerridon. "The One Who Burns will be your undoing. And your end."

The Old Seer's words slipped through his head, spoken over a decade ago but as clear as if only just uttered.

Teeth ground, he turned, fixing his stare on the child standing in the room's entryway. She held the training sword in her right hand—a long, broad blade of hybrid tempered steel with a core of compressed actinide—as if she'd been born with it in her grasp, her chin jutted in stubborn defiance, her green-gold eyes glinting with uncertainty.

He skimmed his gaze over her coiled perfection, partially hidden by her attire, his throat squeezing tighter still as the memory of her wet, glistening body smashed into his mind.

She's not a child, Kerridon. She's never been a child. No matter how hard you try to fool yourself otherwise, she is a woman.

Ignoring the all-too-alluring thought, he gave her a curt nod. "Hand-to-hand. You need to learn how to defeat your enemies with only your hands and feet. How to use your body to bring about their demise."

An ambiguous light flickered in her gaze and he saw her breasts rise with a sudden intake of breath. "Use my body..." She trailed away, catching her bottom lip with her teeth.

The sight sent a shard of something hot and thick into Torin's gut. Syunna, he wanted to bite that lip. Bite it, nibble on it, suck it. He sank his nails harder into his palms, keeping his feet planted to the floor. "We begin," he instructed, readying himself for what was to come next. "Attack me."

The fire in Kala's eyes flared brighter. She stared at him, a frown pulling at her eyebrows. The muscles in her arms and shoulders flexed, the sword's tip swaying a fraction at her feet. He saw her swallow, once, twice.

"Tell me why you need me."

Her calmly spoken command took him by surprise. He narrowed his eyes, his thumping heartbeat leaping into his closed throat. "Do you ignore my order, Kala Rei? Attack me."

She shook her head. "Tell me why you need me first. Why you need me on your ship with you. Why you took me from Earth."

"You know this, Kala Rei. The One Who Burns must take possession of the Sun Sword before the False Fire."

Her stare remained fixed on his. "Why?"

She'd asked about the False Fire more than once. He'd never answered her.

"Why?"

The question was sharp, and yet Torin's pulse quickened at the hint of frustrated desperation in its single syllable. "If the

False Fire takes the Immortals' blade before the One Who Burns, the worlds of man will suffer untold agony."

If she was shocked by his sudden divulgement of information she did not show it. "Is that the only reason?" Her stare never wavered from his face. "A sword in someone's hands?"

He bit back his own frustration. "It is not just a sword, Kala. And the False Fire is not just 'someone'." He paused, his mouth dry. "*You* are not just 'someone'."

She stood motionless. "Who am I then, Torin Kerridon? To you?"

He looked at her, keeping his face free of expression. "You are the One Who Burns."

Her lips parted at the title and she flicked her tongue over their soft fullness before giving him an unreadable stare. "Then tell me, who do I burn for?"

Me.

The word almost fell from Torin's mouth before he could stop it. He growled, letting Kala see his contemptuous anger. Gods pray that she believed it directed at her. "Attack me now, wielder of the Sun Sword, or I will break your back and spit on your pain."

Disgust flooded her face. Misery shone in her eyes. She threw her training sword aside and ran at him, her knuckles white. As always, her speed astounded him, her natural grace arousing him. She feigned left, her right arm swinging into a wide arc, as if to smash her fist into his jaw, just as she dropped into a low spin and punched her left heel into his gut.

Or would have, if he'd not snatched her ankle mid-air and flipped her onto her back.

She slammed onto the floor, the wind bursting from her in

a choked grunt. He grabbed her calf with his other hand, his grip on her ankle tightening as he twisted her leg until she lay half on her side, half on her belly. "Too obvious, Kala," he stated, looking down her leg into her face. The pain he saw in her eyes made his chest ache with guilt and regret, but he denied it power. "And too slow. You will need to do better before I give you what you want."

Her jaw clenched, her eyes becoming heavy-lidded. "What I want." She jackknifed her body, using his hold on her leg to act as a counter pivot, slicing her other leg up into a swift arc as she slammed down into the side of his knee. He buckled, red-hot pain lashing up his leg into his hip and gut. Kala didn't hesitate. She twisted in his grip, smacking her shin against his calf. New pain detonated in his knee but he switched it off, flinging her onto her stomach with a savage flick of her leg and ramming his foot between her shoulder blades.

"You are better than this, Kala Rei." His gut squirmed, as it did every training session, the thought of causing her any harm like blades dipped in acid slicing into his body. "You had me on the ground in half the time back on Earth." He pressed his foot harder to her back, his stare fixed on her profile as she struggled beneath his pinning hold. "What is on your mind to stop you doing so again?"

"You," she snarled.

His heart stopped, his whole body stilling.

She took advantage of his aberrant hesitation, twisting on the floor to smash her elbow into his ankle. The blow would have been awkward, ineffectual—*if* he'd been focused on holding her to the ground with his foot.

He stumbled forward, the pain in his knee bursting with new white heat as his full weight crashed down on it.

Kala was on her feet in a second, slamming her heel into

the small of his back. He careened several steps forward, new pain detonating up his spine. It sank into the base of his skull before, with the same preternatural speed that kept him alive through umpteen bloody battles, he flung himself into a deep cartwheel and swung his foot upward, straight into her chin.

She arched backward, arms flailing. Before she could regain her balance, he rammed his body into hers, his blood roaring in his ears. He drove her backward until she slammed against the training room's cold metal wall. De-atomizers, gutting blades, pulse pistols and twin scythes jolted from their hooks, clattering to the floor in a jarring cacophony. Torin didn't care. His hands curled into fists around Kala's wrists and he pinned her to the wall, his stare fixed on her wide, stunned eyes. "Concentrate," he snapped, a carnal fire igniting in his groin at the feel of her firm softness pressed against him. "Stop thinking of me and think of your training."

"I can't."

Pulse growing fast, he closed his fists harder around her wrists, glaring at her. "Can't what, Kala Rei?"

"I can't stop thinking about you."

The fire in Torin's groin erupted at her blunt confession. He gazed down into her face, felt her heart thumping behind her breast, a rapid beat that sent waves of vibrations into his body. Pulling in a sharp breath, he tasted her sweat on the air. Tasted the musk of a desire he never dreamt possible there too.

He dropped his stare to her mouth, to the lips he'd longed to claim for what felt like an eternity. The tip of her tongue flicked out, wet them, the action so quick Torin doubted Kala even knew she'd done it. Fresh blood surged into his cock, turned it into a rigid length grinding against her belly. She shifted beneath him, pushing her hips forward. Aligning her sex closer to his erection.

Syunna, take her. Take her now!

The deafening order roared through his head. He gazed at her mouth. Felt her body against his. Smelt her musk on the air. Tasted it on his breath.

Take her!

He shoved himself away from her, the abrupt absence of her heat on his flesh, against his body, was like an icy burn. Heart smashing in his throat, his balls and cock harder than steel, he turned his back on her, refusing to look at her face. By the gods, what was wrong with him? He'd given her his word. He'd sworn he would not touch her so. He'd sworn he would never—

"Coward."

He froze, Kala's flat whisper stabbing into him. Infuriating him. Igniting him. He spun, hands snaring her wrists before she could move, slamming her to the wall, his hips and thighs pinning her beneath his weight. He stared down into her face, denying the panic he saw there, every molecule in his body brittle, strained to breaking point. "I am no coward, Kala Rei."

Her lips parted. To say what, he didn't know. Or care. Not when she felt so soft and firm against his body.

He couldn't fight himself any longer. He crushed her mouth with his, forcing her legs apart with his knees before rubbing his right one against the junction of her thighs. Her soft heat scalded his flesh through the course leather of his trousers and he growled, the sound rumbling up his chest into his throat. Kala's lips parted to the noise, her low whimper flooding his groin with potent need as she met his tongue with hers.

His head swam. He dragged his hands down her arms, down her ribcage, plunging his tongue deeper into her mouth as he grabbed the cheeks of her arse and yanked her sex to his straining cock. She arched against him, sliding her arms around his shoulders, tangling her fingers in his hair. Another whimper escaped her and she rolled her hips, pressing her spread sex firmer against his knee.

Torin groaned, raking one hand from her arse to cup and squeeze her breast, the fire in the pit of his gut, his groin, his chest, borderline frantic. He captured her nipple, the subtle snakeskin of her vest doing nothing to hide the puckered hardness from his touch.

Another wave of raw giddiness flooded his head. His touch. He pulled her closer. He was touching her. Really touching her.

Stop it. Now.

He shut the voice out, dragging his mouth from her lips to score a line along her jaw, up to her ear. She rolled her head, offering her throat to his mouth. He nipped the delicate flesh beneath her ear, pressed his tongue to the wild pulse there. She groaned, a low hitching sound unlike any he'd heard her make before and she closed her hands tighter in his hair, as if she feared letting him go.

"I will never let you go, Kala," he murmured into her ear, nipping at her earlobe with his teeth. "You are—"

Mine.

The word whispered through Torin's head, possessive and dominating.

Uncontrolled.

He froze, the inferno in his core extinguished immediately. Syunna, what was he doing? He was *Sol*, keeper of the Sun Sword's truth, not possessor of the One Who Burns. His job was to train her, prepare her, not use her for his own carnal gratification.

He lifted his head and stared down into her heavy-lidded eyes.

Eyes that grew wider the farther he drew away from her. Eyes that shimmered with confusion, disbelief. Pain.

Anger.

He took a step backward, his whole body—not just his groin but his gut, his chest, his throat—aching from what he was doing. What he was about to do.

His solemn oath from six months ago came back to him: "*I will never stick my dick between your legs.*" The words haunted him. An oath he'd made the first time he'd pressed his body to hers, before he'd known who she was. What she was. His gut churned. "Kala..."

She stared at him, an emotionless mask falling over her face.

A second before she smashed her fist into his jaw.

Zroya Gr'h stood over the naked female cowering at his feet on the floor of her bedroom, his gaze tracing the bowed curve of her spine, the toe of his boot tracing the swell of her compressed breast. His dick grew hard in his trousers and he chuckled, dropping into a crouch beside her sniveling form. "Tell me where the Sun Sword is, cunt, and I will not hurt you." He skimmed the palm of his hand over her trembling shoulders, the heat from her body warming his flesh. She shuddered, flinching from his closeness. He *tsked*, moving his hand up to her head, following the delicate curve of her skull. She was a pretty young thing—small, petite, her creamy brown skin like smooth velvet, her thick black hair like a cascading river of midnight ink. Tilting his head to the side, he snatched a handful of that glossy curtain and smashed her face into the floor.

She cried out, fighting against him, scratching at his hold, but he pressed harder on the back of her head, ignoring her feeble attempts to escape. He *tsked* again, giving her a pitying smile. "Tell me where the Sun Sword is, False Fire, or I will break every bone in your body and fuck you until you drown in your own blood."

The stupid female screeched and bucked and thrashed. "I don't know. I'm not... I'm..." She blubbered on and on, professing ignorance, her cries growing choked and gurgled as the stone beneath her head turned bright red.

His cock stiffened further and he flicked his gaze down the line of her back to her arse. His mouth filled with saliva and he grinned. "I shall take you in the arse first, I think. Pump you full of my seed. Would you like that? Bury myself in your arse until you scream for mercy."

She sobbed and bucked again, scratching at his hand. "Don't...gods, please, don't, don't!"

"Enough!" a dry, low voice cracked.

Zroya jerked his stare from the female's backside and snapped his attention to the old man standing in the doorway on the other side of the dimly lit room. He frowned, chest heavy, holding his tongue even as he held the fistful of cool, silken hair in his grip.

The old man took a step forward, white eyes narrowing. His tongue flicked out in rapid succession, tasting the air. He stood motionless for a long moment, a cloudy fog filling his eyes, his expression blank. Empty. "She is not the one, Zroya." He cast the sobbing girl a look devoid of connection. "This is not the False Fire you seek."

Zroya bared his teeth, the proclamation sending a jagged spear of sheer fury into his gut. Not the False Fire. Which meant the useless female would not know the location of that destined to be his.

Fuck.

He studied the old man before him, the rage at his wasted time twisting through the abject reverence and fear he felt for the prophet. "What shall I do with her, master, if she is not the one we seek?"

The old man turned, his long black coat stitched with intricate silver thread flaring into a wide arc, revealing a glimpse of fine silver-mesh trousers and two skinned, bloody rabbit corpses hanging from his belt. "I care little, Zroya," he answered over his shoulder. With a limping gait, he stepped from the doorway into another part of the female's home, lost to Zroya's sight. "Enjoy yourself."

The last command floated to Zroya's ears and his lips spread into a pleased smile, his stare returning to the almost lifeless woman's naked form once again. "Yes, master," he murmured.

With infinite care, he removed his hand from her hair, gently sliding his fingertips past the bloody mess of her face to tuck them under her wet, tacky chin. Raising her head, he gazed into her swollen eyes. "Pl-please," she sobbed, snot and blood pissing from her shattered nose. "Please don't...hurt me."

Zroya showed her his teeth in a wide smile. "I must do what my master tells me to do, *pl'yat*." He smashed his fist into her nose, grinning at the fountain of blood erupting from its ruptured hole. "I will enjoy myself."

He rose to his feet and slammed his boot into her neck, sending her backward in a limp arc, following her progression with his gaze as she slid across the floor with a thud. In two steps he closed the distance between them, standing over her, his dick hard, his breath even. "Until my master tells me he has found the False Fire, the cunt who dares pretend to be the wielder of the Immortals' blade, who dares hold what is rightfully mine, I will enjoy myself." He lifted his right foot and placed it on the other side of her body, against her hipbone, looking down at her with another pitying smile. "With you."

He moved his hands to the buckle at his waist, his smile turning into a serene grin. "Until it is the False Fire beneath me, submitting to me, you shall accept my wrath. The wrath of the One Who Burns." He gave the pathetic blubbering female a slow wink. "Aren't you lucky."

Chapter Two

The bastard didn't fall.

Kala glared at the cursed *Sol* warrior, her knuckles burning with white pain, her shoulder throbbing with dull heat. She shook her head, biting back the bitter sob threatening to escape her. The hardest punch she could throw and he didn't even flinch. Sour self-disgust and contempt curdled in her belly. She turned her head, unable to look at him, to see him—the cause of her humiliation—any longer. "I am leaving."

He didn't respond to her flat statement, at least not aloud. Kala pushed herself from the wall, chest feeling like it was about to be crushed by an imploding quasar, her throat so tight she could barely breathe. She turned back to him, risking one last look before she got the hell off his ship. She was done with this shit.

He stood before her, motionless, expression revealing nothing, his eyes unreadable. The only sign something bothered him was the coiled steel in his muscles and the bunching of his jaw.

Something? What, like rejecting you? He is the last command warrior of the Sol *Order, Kala. Keeper of the Sun fucking Sword's truth. Do you really think he cares he's just ripped your heart from your chest and crushed it beneath his heel?*

Hot hate cut through her and, fists clenched, she shoved

past him, scooping her sword up from the floor and storming from the training room. Her body ached—not from the physical beating Torin had given her, but from the physical hunger he'd denied it.

Christ, Kala. You are a bloody fool.

Gut twisting, she headed for her quarters, willing the ache deep within her core to go away. She needed to gather her things and—

A cold emptiness flooded through her and she faltered to a halt, her lips prickling with numb grief. Her things? What things? She didn't have any *things*. What she stood in now was all she possessed in this world.

The heavy weight in her hand drew her tormented attention and she lowered her head, gazing at the training sword still in her grasp. She snarled, throwing it aside, the coldness in her being turning to icy disgust. It didn't belong to her. All it was was a poor imitation of a weapon she was never intended to hold, a ludicrous myth spoken of in hushed tones by idiots who believed the worlds of man had once been better than they were now.

The Sun Sword. A weapon as powerful as the sun itself. Kala shook her head, the bile in the back of her throat hot. As if such a sword existed.

As if she—an abandoned earthling with no memory of her past before puberty—was the one born to wield it.

And yet, you'd almost begun to believe Torin's bullshit. You almost believed you had a purpose. Worth. That your existence meant something to someone.

Biting back a growl of self-contempt, she started walking again, heading toward *Helios Blade*'s hull. For six months the deep-space class vessel had been her home. She knew every inch of its interior, every item within its structure, including the small inter-star skip nestled in its bowel. The streamline short-range shuttle may only get her one hyper-jump away from Torin Kerridon, but that was one hyper-jump farther than where she was now.

Far enough to forget how stupid she'd been. How monumentally naive.

And if he follows you?

Kala curled her fists. A lifetime of pain and fear, of being hunted by the animals calling themselves men on Earth's surface had taught her one thing—how to become invisible. If she didn't want him to, the *Sol* warrior would never find her.

Who are you kidding, Kala? If Torin Kerridon wanted to find you, he would. If he wanted to find you.

Dull pain blossomed in her chest at the thought and she quickened her pace, shutting all emotions down as she hurried to the shuttle bay. Emotions were a weakness she couldn't afford.

The shuttle bay door was locked when she arrived, the passageway leading to it dark. Floor lights flickered into muted life as she stepped onto the grid, casting a dull yellow glow around her feet that barely penetrated the blackness. She fumbled with the locking mechanism, her heart hammering in her ears. The back of her neck itched, as if someone watched her, his stare unseen in the shrouding darkness but felt all the same.

Torin?

Kala's throat squeezed tight at the sound of his name in her head, her sex fluttering in traitorous response. She threw a quick look over her shoulder, squinting into the dense shadows.

The blackness devoured her sight and, frowning, she turned back to the locking panel. Torin wasn't there. He would not expect her to be here. His arrogance would have him believe she had returned to her quarters after their exchange in the training room, sulking over what happened. His unending belief in the Sun Sword and her role as the savior of mankind would not allow him to imagine her words "I'm leaving" to mean anything but leaving the training session.

Besides, she couldn't detect his distinct scent on the stale, still air.

She levered open the panel, the lack of light making the task difficult, the continuing itch on the back of her neck making her want to fidget. The sensation of being watched grew stronger, heavier. She shot another furtive look over her shoulder, almost expecting to see someone standing directly behind her.

Nothing.

Just blackness.

"You're going mad, Kala," she muttered, scanning the lock's internal components with her fingertips. The low thrum of *Helios Blade*'s engines tickled the soles of her feet and the pit of her belly, making the task more difficult than it should. The itch continued and she ground her teeth against its inescapable annoyance. Just her mind playing tricks on her, that's all. Just her screwed up, masochistic mind trying to mess with her. Prevent her doing what she had to do—leave.

Finding what she hoped was the releasing mechanism, she activated its function. A sharp breath of relief burst from her as the door slid open. She hurried inside, the shuttle bay lights automatically switching on as she crossed the short distance to the sleeping skip.

Harsh white light flooded the bay and she blinked, her eyes reacting to the sudden illumination. Without thought, her body coiled into readiness. Close to two hundred days of Torin's unrelenting training so much a part of who she was now, she was ready to fight before being aware of it. She dashed around the skip's pointed bow on silent feet, the scowl on her face feeling strained, the weight on her chest and in her sex feeling numb. Reaching the vessel's sole hatch, she rested her palm on its locking release.

This was it. Two minutes to power up, thirty seconds to open the shuttle bay doors, two seconds to blast the hell away from Torin Kerridon.

And then what? Keep running? Keep hiding?

Kala closed her eyes, her stomach churning. Yes. Keep running. What other option did she have?

No matter how well you hide, he will find you. He will come after you.

Pressing her forehead to the cold steel hatch, Kala caught her bottom lip with her teeth. Torin *would* come after her, but not for the reasons she wished he would.

The pulse in her neck thumped hard, and she let out a groaning hiss. She had to go. She had to.

But you're not. Are you?

Pressing her hand flat against the hatch release, she opened her eyes and stared at the side of the skip.

Are you?

Barely able to draw breath, she straightened away from the skip and turned.

Torin stood directly behind her, his grey eyes haunted, his face carved from stone. "Don't go."

She stared at him, her heart slamming into her throat. "Okay."

His nostrils flared at her simple response and, with the same preternatural strength she's seen so many times in the training room, he wrapped his arms around her waist and

43

Lexxie Couper

yanked her to his body, his mouth claiming hers with furious savagery.

Raw and rapturous pleasure consumed her. She gave herself to the kiss, raking her hands up his strong, hard arms, the back of his neck, tangling her fingers in the thick softness of his hair. Every molecule in her body sang with joy. She pushed herself closer to his firmness, wanting to feel every inch of him against her. With a low growl and a quick tightening of his embrace, he slid his hands to her arse and hauled her from the floor.

She wrapped her legs around his hips, locked her ankles behind his back and rolled her sex over the length of his trapped erection. The friction sent exquisite ribbons of squeezing heat into her core and she moaned.

Torin reacted to the low sound. His tongue plunged deeper into her mouth, flicked at her teeth. He bit on her bottom lip, sucked the bruise with gentle pressure, his hands cupping her arse, a low, primal groan rumbling in his chest.

Yes yes yes yes!

The inane word repeated itself in Kala's mind, growing faster, more feverish with each hard caress of Torin's hands, with every stabbing flick of his tongue in her mouth. She rolled her hips, bowing her back to grind her pussy to his cock. Its massive length punished her soft folds, even through the leather of their trousers and she reveled in the pleasure. He'd followed her. He wanted her. Not for what he believed her to be, but for what she was—a woman.

His woman.

Yes, his woman. His.

Tearing her mouth from his, she gave him her neck, wanting to feel his lips and teeth scoring the sensitive flesh there. He complied, raining a scalding trail of wild kisses up to

44

the little dip behind her ear, down to the curve of her shoulder and back to her jaw again, sending a ripple of concentrated delight through her.

"By the gods, I should not crave you like this," he murmured against her cheek, his voice tortured. "This is not what the Old Seer foresaw."

Who gives a fuck what some old bloke saw? Kala wanted to say, but the words wouldn't come, asphyxiated by the exquisite pleasure consuming her. She closed her eyes, whimpering as Torin's lips returned to her ear. He traced the shallow inner shell with the tip of his tongue, the wet caress making her pussy constrict and the pit of her belly twist. She arched her back again, pressing her sex to his rock-hard cock, thrusting her breasts forward. Please, she wanted to beg. Please take me.

As if hearing her unspoken plea, Torin pressed her against the side of the skip and spread his legs enough to support her weight. Staring into her eyes, nostrils flaring, he slid his hands from her arse, raking them over her hips, up her ribcage to the swell of her breasts. "Syunna, forgive me," he whispered on a hoarse breath, before hooking his fingers beneath the edge of her vest and yanking the snakeskin apart.

Her breasts tumbled free, only to be claimed immediately by his strong hands.

He captured her nipples between his fingers, pinched them with a gentle force that mocked the inferno in his eyes.

"Yes!" Kala moaned, liquid electricity shooting through her core. She bucked, the raw pleasure from Torin's touch flooding her pussy with tight heat.

"Syunna, Kala, you are beautiful." He yanked her farther up his body, the sodden junction of her thighs sliding up the flatness of his abdomen until, with a groan both angry and desperate, he closed his lips around one peaked nipple and sucked on it. Hard.

Ribbons of pure ecstasy knotted in her core. She cried out, arching her spine more, holding his head still. Her sex constricted, flooded with moisture. He growled around her nipple and bit down on it with his teeth, his thumb and forefinger treating the puckered tip of her other breast with equal ferocity. Kala gasped, something molten and heavy building between her legs. The soles of her feet tingled. Her heart hammered.

Christ, what was happening?

Torin suckled harder, teasing with tongue and teeth and lips, the rhythm of his mouth in perfect harmony with the increasing flutters in her cunt. She threw back her head, staring with blank wonder and terror at the grey metal ceiling. The tension mounting in her very centre grew tighter. Her sex constricted, pulsing in erratic waves. Each throb made her gasp, as if something beyond her understanding tried to render her defenseless. Unmade. She sucked in a swift breath, the constricting throb radiating through her body. Consuming her. God, what was happening? Oh, God, what was Torin doing to her?

She squirmed in his hold, the squeezing heat building, growing heavier, tighter. She fisted his hair, rolled her eyes, her breath rapid, shallow. The pressure in her centre spread, grew thicker. Came in mounting waves of liquid fire.

Oh...oh...what...what...

Torin tore his left hand from her breast and, with a groan that was more a guttural growl, he plunged it between their bodies, sinking his fingers into her folds in one fluid move.

He scissored them inside her sex, wriggled them deeper, his mouth still sucking on her breast, his tongue still lathing her nipple.

"Oh, oh." Her strangled gasp ripped from her raw throat. She writhed in his arms, blank stare fixed on the bay's ceiling, her teeth pulling at her bottom lip. Control. She was losing—

"Fuck," Torin ground against her breast, cupping it with savage fingers. "I want you, Kala. I want you so fucking much I am in agony." He shoved his hips higher, the thick length of his erection grinding high against her inner thigh a testament to his words. "I want...I want..." His mouth scored a fierce path to her other breast and he took her nipple with his lips and teeth, suckling so hard, shooting tendrils of pain laced through her pleasure.

She whimpered, the pain unlike any she knew—wicked and intoxicating and potent. She wanted to experience it again. She wanted him to stop. To let her catch her breath. To regain control. She wanted to lose control. She wanted...

Torin mauled her breast with his hand and sucked her nipple again, his feral groan vibrating through his chest into the pit of her belly.

Oh...oh...

Her pussy throbbed, heavy with incomprehensible heat.

Oh, God, what is...

Torin drove his fingers deeper, burying them into that heavy, gripping heat. Stroked the inner walls of her sex with unrelenting force.

She bucked against him, the tiny button hidden in her folds grinding against the base knuckle of his fingers. Liquid electricity shot through her. Her pulse pounded in her neck and she whimpered again, closing her eyes. Christ, she felt like she was going to—

Torin's mouth tore from her breast and, his chest having, he gazed into her eyes. "What have you done to me, Kala? Gods, I've never hungered for something as much as I..."

He didn't finish and she couldn't blame him. How could she when she was incapable of speech herself? Incapable of understanding what was happening to her, let alone Torin?

Another raw groan rumbled in his chest and he dropped his head to her breast again, closing his lips around her aching nipple and suckling once more.

She arched her back, the brief moment of damned, torturous respite over, her body burning hotter with every drawing sensation Torin's mouth wrought on her breast. With every plunging thrust of his fingers.

He shifted his hand—barely a fraction—and new pleasure rushed through her as he pressed his fingertips to the inside wall of her sex. Hot pleasure. Wet pleasure.

"Oh, Kala," he moaned against her breast. "You are so tight. So tight and so fucking wet." He shoved his fingers higher, deeper into her folds and bit down on her nipple.

Clamping, contracting tension detonated through Kala's centre. She screamed, the exquisite, terrifying sensation taking possession of every muscle of her body. She thrashed in Torin's embrace, unable to think, to control herself. Waves of choking pleasure crashed over her, tore through her. She cried out, control deserting her. Each shudder, each contraction of her sex around Torin's penetrating fingers crashed through her like an exploding star, stealing her ability to exist.

Pleasure claimed her. Terror following instantly. She couldn't stop it. She couldn't control it. It felt so good but she was drowning in it, losing control. Losing *her*.

It's too much. Too much. Oh, God, it feels so good, so...

The shudders grew faster, stronger, the heavy tension tighter. She rolled her head, unable to comprehend what was happening to her. Her breath grew shorter, her pulse pounding, her body fighting the raw, wild sensations consuming it.

Too much, I can't, I can't, stop, stop.

She writhed in Torin's hold, against his thrusting fingers, the crotch of her trousers sodden with moisture, her sex thick with pulsing pressure. She couldn't control herself. She couldn't control her body. She couldn't...she couldn't...

Oh, God, it's too much, it's too much, I can't, I can't, I—

"Can't, no, no, stop, stop, *stop!*"

Her cry ripped from her throat, loud and rent with fear.

And Torin stiffened, his head jerking from her breast, his fingers stilling in her sex.

He stared at her, stunned disbelief flooding his face before, with a snarl of absolute disgust, he threw her out of his arms and stormed from the shuttle bay. Without a word or backward glance.

Kala stared at the gaping doorway, her body still claimed by the shudders of her overwhelming pleasure. She slumped against the skip's metal hull. Its icy surface scalded her flushed flesh, but she didn't care. She welcomed the physical pain. It was something she understood, something she knew.

Her heart pounded with cruel force, crushed by Torin's brutal desertion and yet still beating. Still keeping her alive.

He'd left her. Torin had left her. The only man to ever give her pleasure, the only man she ever wanted to do so and he'd walked way from her.

She fell to her knees, her stare locked on the empty shuttle bay door, her breath caught in her throat. God, he'd left her alone. What did she do now?

What in the name of Syunna are you doing?

Torin stormed through his ship, barely controlling the urge to smash his fists against the metal walls. He headed for the cockpit, his body so charged with disgusted loathing he felt like someone had stuck a blade into his gut. By the gods, he was a monster.

Torin Kerridon, last command warrior of the Sol *Order. Keeper of the Sun Sword's truth.*

Rapist.

He drove his blunt nails into his palms and slammed open the cockpit door, punching a sequence into the navi-comp and dropping into the captain's chair.

Rapist.

The heinous word rolled through his head like diseased fog, sickening him. He ground his teeth, his gut churning. The one thing he'd sworn to Kala before taking her from Earth, the one thing he'd promised—never to stick his dick between her legs— and he'd come so close to destroying that oath.

He stared out at the never-ending blackness of deep space, Kala's cries reverberating through his head, an endless loop he couldn't silence or ignore. He'd thought them cries of pleasure. He'd thought them the sounds of her release. His blood had been roaring in his ears, his own pleasure so absolute at finally being with her the way he'd longed that he'd been deafened to her terror.

Can't, no, no, stop, stop, stop!

Kala screamed in his head again and he let out a choked sob, dropping his face into his hands.

Syunna, what had he done?

You know what you've done. You lost control. Forgot who you are. Forgot who she is. The question is what are you going to do now?

50

What *did* he do now?

Leave her alone. Let her have some space.

Let her climb aboard the skip and leave.

He let out a sharp growl, slamming his fist onto the control deck. By the gods, he couldn't let her do that. He couldn't let her leave.

Why? Because you haven't had your fill of her yet?

Contemptuous disgust coated his mouth at the vile question and he shook his head. No. Because she was the One Who Burns. The fate of mankind rested on her tiny body. In her hands, the Sun Sword would end the rise of malevolence destroying the known universes. In her hands, the Immortals' blade would bring light where there was only dark.

What does that mean? You have spent the entire thirty-four years of your life believing an ambiguous notion told by an old man who claimed to see it in the stars. Every aspect of who you are has been built around a prophecy that makes no gods-cursed sense. What if the whole thing is a lie? What if the Sun Sword doesn't exist at all? What if—

Torin smashed his fists onto the control deck again, his snarl of furious frustration gouging at his throat. No. He could not believe that. The *Sol* were older than any other warriors in the known universes. They were the guardians and protectors of the known universes' one true weapon. They were selected at birth, trained from that moment. They were the most feared and hunted soldiers to live. Men selected by the Oracle for their infinite, violent rage, a furious power controlled and contained by disciplined faith. If the Sun Sword and the prophecy were all a fabrication then what was the meaning of his own existence?

"You, Torin Kerridon, are the last of the Sol *now. All your brother warriors have been butchered."* The Old Seer's voice echoed through his head, a blunt declaration from a decade

51

ago. His jaw bunched and his fists squeezed tighter. *"It is your task and your task alone to find and ready the One Who Burns. No one else must do this. If you do not, the False Fire will prevail. If you do not, all will be lost."*

The Old Seer had never questioned the prophecy. No matter how cruel and demanding and ambiguous the words that came to him in his visions, the old man had remained true.

"As you *must, Kerridon."*

Opening his eyes, Torin stared out the cockpit viewscreen. If he was to question his belief now, did he do so solely because of his dangerous desire for Kala Rei? He'd never questioned his role in the prophecy before—he'd seen too many predicted events unfold, too many brutal deaths and travesties committed in the name of the Sun Sword. He existed for one thing and one thing only—to see the ultimate weapon in the hands of the ultimate warrior. Did he turn his back on that existence now? In the hands of the False Fire—the one the Old Seer foretold would hunger the sword with murderous intent—the Immortal's blade was an instrument of death. Did he deny everything he knew and pray the prophecy was nothing but a lie?

Life. Death.

The beginning of the future or the end of existence.

All hanging in the balance because he couldn't keep his desire for Kala Rei under cursed control.

He dragged his hands through his hair, the dull ache in his knuckles telling him he'd hit the control deck harder than he should. "Good," he snarled, shifting in his seat as he adjusted the co-ordinates of *Helios Blade*'s trajectory. Pain was good. He deserved to feel it.

Pushing himself from his chair, he activated the auto-pilot and left the cockpit, heading for the training room.

He *needed* to feel pain. More pain.

A lot of pain.

Zroya strode across the marbled centre court of the Solaris Nuns' compound on P'helios Prime, the squirming weight he dragged behind him impeding his speed not one micro-second.

"Let me go, you fuck!" the weight screamed, scratching at his wrist with torn, ragged, blood-seeping fingernails. "Let me go, let me go, *let me go!*"

"Hush," he soothed over his shoulder. He tightened his grip on the female's long dark hair, his gaze never wavering from his master standing motionless on the temple steps.

The prophet's white eyes were closed, his leathery face slack and reposed.

"Let me go!" the Solaris slut pretending to be the One Who Burns screeched. She thrashed, her broken legs flopping uselessly against the smooth marble floor.

Zroya curled his lip. The False Fire had tried to defend herself against his unexpected attack by kicking him. Kicking *him.* Striking out at his groin with her feet when he'd wrapped his hands around her neck and squeezed.

He'd punished her for her stupidity, of course, smashing his fist to her nose, shattering both her knees with his heels. The squeals of her pain flooded his groin with hot lust and he'd almost mounted her there and then. But for his master waiting in the temple.

There were preparations to be made before he could subjugate the False Fire. Rituals to perform. After those rituals, however...

A tight spasm shot through Zroya's cock. "Then we shall

have our fun, False Fire."

"Let me go, you dumb fuck!" the writhing, scratching, thrashing female screeched, clawing at his wrist. "I'm not—"

"Hush," he said again, snapping his arm forward. "Your language is unacceptable."

The female screamed, her hands scrambling at his fist in her hair.

"Hush or I shall bite the tongue from your mouth."

His blunt promise shut her up. "That is better." Who would have thought a nun would be so troublesome? He chuckled, walking faster, his gaze still locked on his master. Who would have thought the False Fire would be a Solaris Nun? It was an entirely entertaining revelation, however. He'd never fucked a virgin before, let alone one sanctified by the old gods. "Behave yourself and all will be well."

Sniveling sobs followed his lie, the futile struggles ceasing. He nodded. "Much better."

He strode the remaining distance to the temple in silence, his body already prepared for what was to come. Once the Sun Sword was his, well...if the female wanted to scream again, he would not stop her.

"Master." He reached the temple steps and dropped to his knee, dragging the False Fire's face down to the cold marble floor by his foot. "She refuses to give me the Sun Sword or reveal its location."

The prophet, the wise one who had found him as a starving child in the sinful streets of Cortallia, selling his body and mouth to depraved men with depraved hands for a scrap of something to eat, lifted his face to the bruised-purple sky. "She refuses because she does not know."

As always, the stripped-rawness of his master's voice sent

ribbons of bliss through Zroya's being, despite his unexpected statement. "She does not know?" He turned his head to stare at the female shaking with silent sobs on the floor beside him.

"I told you I—" she began to shriek, bulging eyes streaming blood and tears.

He slammed her face against the marble and she stopped.

"I have seen her."

His master's calm statement struck Zroya hard and he jerked his stare up. "Seen?"

The prophet tilted his head to the side, long white hair sliding over his thin shoulder, the stone beads threaded in its strands clattering together in a soft tinkle. "She is on a ship. Within its belly." He rolled his neck, returning his unseeing eyes to Zroya's face. "She is..." a small smile played with the corners of his mouth and Zroya barely suppressed his rapturous cringe. When his master smiled, pain ensued. White, cleansing pain. "She is angry."

Snapping to his feet, Zroya gazed into the prophet's face. "Where?"

His master's eyelids fluttered and he stroked the rotting rabbits on his belt, the clotting blood sticking to the tips of his fingers. "Close."

Hot wire curled into a knot in Zroya's gut and he stiffened. Close. His balls grew heavy, his fists clenched. He flicked a glance at the thing on the floor at his feet. Close.

A hot hiss sliced the air and he jerked his stare back to his master, stepping back a step at the expression the prophet wore. Fury. And fear. "Master?"

"She is not alone." His master's tongue flicked past his lips, his white eyes fixed on the space directly above Zroya's head. The seams in his leathery face etched deeper, and he hissed again, the sound unlike any Zroya had heard him make. "She is with—" He stopped and spun about, robe swirling, the cloying stench of the rotting rabbits rolling from him in a thick wave as he walked up the temple steps.

Zroya blinked, his master's behavior surprising him. Did he follow? Did he wait?

"Kill the female," the prophet's shout rose above the hiccuping sobs at his ankle. "And bring her heart. There is much to be learned before we find the False Fire."

Zroya watched his master hurry away, an uncomfortable tension twisting in his belly. Who or what would make his master scared?

"Wh-what are..." the bleeding thing at his feet gurgled and he blinked, turning his stare from his master's back to the female on the floor.

"What am I going to do with you?" he finished for her with a grin. "Well, now the fun begins."

For some reason, the bleeding, broken thing began to scream.

It wasn't enough. Torin's sweat stung his eyes like acid, his body ached with fatigue, every sinew, every muscle worked beyond their physical limit and still it wasn't enough.

He stood in the centre of the training room, head bowed, perspiration dripping from his chin, the tip of his nose, turning the mat at his feet the dark metallic stain of old blood.

He didn't know what to do next. For the first time in his life, he didn't know what to do. Go to Kala? Beg her forgiveness? Leave her alone? Hand her a gutting blade and tell her to sink it into his stomach?

He closed his eyes, the pain in his body was nothing compared to the torture in his soul. He didn't know. He just didn't—

The soft hiss of the entryway door behind him made him freeze.

Silence followed the mechanical sound, nothing audible indicating Kala had entered the training area. But he knew she had. Not just because the room's still, artificial air shifted about him, not just because the almost imperceptible vibrations from her feather-light footfalls rippled up though his legs, but because he was more aware of her than he had any right being.

He didn't move. If she'd come to kill him...

Silence stretched. Grew thicker. Suffocating.

Look at her.

He lifted his head and turned, the knot in his gut twisting tenfold, the icy energy in his muscles at breaking point.

Kala stood but a mere stride behind him, her face composed, her eyes unreadable. In her hand, gripped loosely by slender fingers marred with calluses from countless training sessions, hung the long blade he'd given her in preparation for the Sun Sword, its cold silver length parallel with her right thigh, its pointed tip brushing the bone of her ankle.

He studied her, every molecule in his body straining for her touch, her heat, every atom of his soul despising that craven response. After everything he'd done to her, everything... "Why are you here?" he asked, his voice flat. Unwelcoming.

Kala didn't move. Her expression didn't change. But the knuckles of her right hand, the hand gripping her sword, grew white.

Torin's chest tightened, his body preparing for her attack.

57

And what, Kerridon? Kill or be killed?

He grit his teeth, staring at her.

The One Who Burns will be your undoing. And your end.

Was this the end of which the Old Seer spoke? He had trained her well. She was an instrument of death, a natural warrior in the deceptive guise of a young, vulnerable woman. With hate in her soul, powering her blows and strikes, he doubted the fight would last long. He would be dead before the sweat beaded on her forehead.

Syunna, I welcome it.

"Why are you here?" he repeated, a sense of calm acceptance flowing over him.

"To train."

Her answer, spoken on a steady breath, filled his heart with elation. And dread.

She was letting him live.

By the gods, how was he to survive?

Chapter Three

The sword swung in a wide arc. Its long blinding-gold blade carved the blackness of the night in two, leaving behind concentrated fire and infinite energy. It sang as it did so, a thrum so deep and elemental, so powerful and potent, Torin felt the veins in his body quiver.

He dived away from its lethal trajectory, crashing to his shoulder and rolling across the cold, granite floor, hot pain engulfing his neck and torso as he snapped to his feet and spun about.

She came at him again, hate in her green eyes, the gold circling her pupil aglow with the contemptuous emotion. The sword blurred in her confident grip, a deadly extension of her smooth, brown arm and, before he realized what she was doing, its blinding point sliced up his chest, cutting him open from nipple to shoulder.

He flailed backward, scalding agony searing through him, his stare locked on her face, her beautiful face, the face he would kill for. The face he would die for.

She threw herself forward into a cartwheel so quickly he didn't see her move before her heel smashed into the bridge of his nose.

No.

He went down to his knees, blood oozing from the gaping

wound in his chest, blood gushing from the shattered protrusion on his face. His own sword, the one he'd used since he was twelve, dropped from his hand, sliding across the floor. Out of his reach. Lost in the shadows. Useless.

"I thank you, Torin Kerridon, last command warrior of the *Sol* Order." Kala Rei looked down at him, her eyes cold and merciless. She leveled the point of the blade at the base of his throat. "For training me so well."

He lifted his chin high. "You are welcome, False Fire," he replied. Seconds before the woman he loved plunged the Sun Sword into his—

Torin jerked awake, eyes wide, heart pounding. By the gods, what was *that?*

He studied the dim surroundings of his quarters, his hands curling into fists, his chest heaving. *Syunna, a dream, just a dream.*

He swung his legs over the side of his bunk, planted his feet on the floor and stood, slamming his palm against the control panel beside his head as he did so.

Instantly the small room flooded with harsh light, stinging his eyes and burning his retinas. He moved to the mirror above the tiny washbasin on the far wall, curling his fingers around the basin's icy rim, his stare coming to rest on his tormented reflection.

False Fire.

His throat squeezed tight and he gripped the basin harder. No. He didn't believe that. It was just a dream. His head was so fucked up, his self-contempt so absolute, his psyche was finding new and more heinous ways to mess with him.

False Fire.

He lifted his hand to the base of his throat and pressed his fingers to the soft flesh just above his collarbone.

The place the Sun Sword had separated his head from his body.

He gazed into the basin's shallow depths, struggling to control his heart rate. Syunna, he was in trouble. More trouble than even the Old Seer had foreseen.

A slight noise—barely audible—pierced Torin's ears and he jerked up his head, his stare locking onto the sight of Kala reflected in the mirror.

Her eyes met his in the glass. "I...heard you shout."

He gazed at her for a long second before returning his attention to the basin. "It was nothing." He spun open the hydro release, watching a stream of cold water splash against the metal bowl. "Return to your quarters. We will be making port at Ati'aina in less than two hours. You will need to be well-rested."

Silence followed his command and his skin prickled. The weight of Kala's focus on his back was like a physical force. He ignored it, bending slightly at the waist, scooping his cupped hands into the icy water in the basin and bringing them up to his face.

"Ati'aina?" There was a pause. "Is that where we collect the Sun Sword?"

Torin squeezed his eyes shut. Syunna, how did she know the Sun Sword wasn't in his possession? He pulled in a deep breath, cold water dripping from his nose and chin. "The Sun Sword is not on Ati'aina," he answered, keeping his voice level. She didn't need to know he didn't know where the Immortal's weapon was. If everything went to plan on the remote spaceport, if the damned Oracle agreed to co-operate, he would. Once he knew the sword's location nothing else mattered except retrieving it.

Nothing. Not his guilt, his self-contempt, his flagging

control.

His desire.

"Will I be allowed to leave *Helios Blade*?"

Her question cut him to the core. "You are not my prisoner, Kala Rei," he growled, straightening from the basin to stare at her in the mirror. "If you wish to move about the spaceport, you may. All I ask is you do so with extreme care and wear a locator cuff on your wrist when you do. Ati'aina is not forgiving to those who relax their guard. It makes your Earth seem like the highest level of Heaven by comparison."

The angry look that flickered across her face made his stomach twist, though whether her anger came from his mention of Earth or the locator cuff he could not tell. The last thing he wanted was Kala roaming the spaceport. Ati'aina was dangerous, filled to the brim with criminals, smugglers, slave traders and spice runners. A young female, alone, seemingly unprotected... She would be a fantasy in the flesh. Waiting to be plucked and devoured.

But you can't confine her to your ship either. Not after—

He cut the thought dead. They had not spoken of the events in *Helios Blade*'s shuttle bay. She'd come to him, they'd trained with the sword, she'd left and he'd returned to his quarters. Not a word had been uttered by either of them. That she still stayed with him, even in this strained, nerve-wrenching capacity, was enough. The worlds of man needed her to do so.

And your dream, Kerridon? False Fire? What did that mean? The Old Seer never told you the One Who Burns would be a female. He never mentioned the all-consuming desire you would feel for her—a pretty gods-cursed important piece of information, don't you think? What if he was wrong? What if—

"I think I can take care of myself."

Kala's soft statement jerked his attention back to the

mirror. A small smile curled the corners of her lips and Torin blinked, his heart immediately leaping into rapid life at the sight.

He gave her a level look, wanting to smile back, wanting to turn around and look at *her*, not just her reflection. Wanting to, but denying that want all the same. He lowered his gaze to the basin instead, dipping his hands into its chilly water. "I know you can. But Ati'aina has a very strict no-weapons policy. You will not be able to carry your sword on the spaceport, nor any other weapon you have trained with." He splashed water on his face. "And do not be fooled by anyone. The most innocent of children can turn out to be the most savage of assassins."

And who are you speaking about now, Kerridon? The corridor urchins on Ati'aina? Or Kala Rei?

He scooped more water into his hands. "I shall let you know when we are about to dock. Return to your quarters and get some more sleep."

Silence followed. Long silence that told him Kala had left. He closed his eyes, curled his fingers around the basin's rim and slumped forward, the battle to keep his distance, to stop himself begging her forgiveness more exhausting than the longest session spent in the *Sol* training pits. Gods, he felt adrift. For the first time in his life he was questioning everything he held true. His faith, his purpose, his motivation.

"I'd never had an orgasm before."

He snapped upright, Kala's calm declaration jolting him to the core. Syunna, she was still there. Still behind him.

He turned, his pulse smashing against his neck, and stared at her standing in the entryway of his quarters.

"I remember little of my life on Earth," she continued, her voice still calm, almost detached, her eyes unreadable. "I have no memory of my childhood years at all, just sensations, ghosts in my head. My earliest memory is of a man holding me to the ground, one hand crushing my neck, the other tearing at my clothes. I have no idea how old I was. Maybe ten." She turned her head away. "That was my life. I had no one to care for me, no one to protect me, and so I protected myself."

She paused, and he saw her eyebrows pull into a slight frown. "That isn't easy when you are a young girl. I lived with an old couple for a while, on an abandoned farm away from the dying cities. They were kind. She read to me, taught me how to read. But then the men came and..." Her frown deepened and she closed her eyes. "I got away after a few days and stayed hidden in the dead buildings, but the men would always find me. Eventually—if I was clumsy stealing into the camps looking for food or clothing to shield myself against the bitter cold, or if they just wanted the sport of hunting me down—they would find me."

She stood silent for a long moment, her face emotionless. Torin drove his nails into his palms, the violent need to tear apart those of whom Kala spoke scorching through his veins. He looked at her, something inside his chest breaking. Something deeper turning black. Dangerous. "I will return to Earth and kill them if you ask."

Kala returned her gaze to his face. She shook her head, the same small smile she'd worn earlier playing with her lips again. "No. They are living their own death. Every minute spent on my dying home planet is punishment enough."

Torin remained silent. His body felt like a taut cable on the verge of snapping. And yet, he couldn't move.

Why was she there? In his quarters? Was it for him?

Don't, Kerridon. That path is fraught with hollow pain.

He swallowed.

Kala's eyes narrowed and she scraped her hands through

the black tumble of her hair. "I've hated you for six months. For six months I've wanted nothing more than to see you dead."

A cold fist reached into Torin's chest.

"Six months of despising you for the physical pain you've put me through." Her green gaze flicked to him, away and back again. "Six months of...of..." She stopped. Shook her head again. Closed her eyes and rubbed at her face with her hands. "Damn you, Torin Kerridon," she muttered into her palms. Jerking her head up, she glared at him. "I'd never had an orgasm until yesterday. Until you touched me. And then you left me alone. Deserted me."

Torin's heart stopped. His breath caught. He stared at her, his blood roaring in his ears, his heart hammering in his throat. Did she...? Was she...? He took a step forward.

For the third time, Kala shook her head. "I will see you when we dock on Ati'aina, Torin."

She turned and left the entryway.

Torin stared at the empty doorway, the skin behind his neck prickling, his nostrils flaring. He curled his fingers into fists with agonizing pressure. It was the only way. The only way to stop himself going after her.

He'd never wanted to do anything as much as he wanted to claim Kala for his own. To scald away her hideous past. Fill her with the rapture of true pleasure. Show her what the pure pleasure of absolute trust and selfless need truly felt like.

Giving her that would give *him* pleasure. Unlike any he dared dream.

He turned back to the basin and the mirror above it, staring at his tortured reflection. He wanted to go to her. Syunna, he wanted to go to her.

But he didn't.

Honour kept his feet still. Kept him in his quarters, blood thick with hope, groin thick with longing. Honour kept him from going to Kala.

Cursed, torturous honour.

Damn it.

Ati'aina spaceport was unlike anything Kala had ever seen. Sprawling common areas made of metal and filled with iridescent lights advertising various businesses, most of them, as far as she could tell, relating in some way to self-gratification. Strip clubs, sex dens, spice bars, all overflowing with patrons, all dimly lit and smelling of sweat, piss and God alone knows what else.

Branching off said common areas, like sinuous limbs, were long passageways, some wide and brightly lit, some narrow and dark. Life forms of every kind moved along their lengths. Kala had never seen so many varied species in the same place. She tried not to stare, but this world was far removed from the insular nightmare of her existence on Earth. Humans freely strode beside aliens she'd never imagined, creatures that looked like they'd just stepped from her nightmares, her fantasies. Creatures of breathtaking beauty and hideous visage. Reptilian beings, cyborgs, beings part-human part-animal. Even creatures that defied description walked beside each other, conversed with each other.

She swiveled her head, doing her best to see it all. She should be scared—she'd never seen anything like it. The only aliens she'd seen on Earth were far more humanoid than most of those moving around her now. She should be at least hyperventilating a little, made nervous by what she saw. But she wasn't. A strange little thrill tickled in her belly and she couldn't stop the grin stretching her lips. A spaceport. She was on a spaceport.

And could you be anymore obvious? You may as well walk around with a sign saying "tourist".

The cynical rebuke made Kala snort and she grinned wider. She'd never stepped foot off Earth until Torin found her, let alone travelled beyond the derelict planet's system. She was allowed to be excited.

But not stupid. Remember what Torin said. This is not a safe haven. This is a dangerous place and you are completely unarmed. The way you're carrying on, you're asking for trouble.

Kala let out a harsh sigh and removed the smile from her face. It was true. She was behaving like a child. She needed to grow up.

Threading her way through the crowd, she scanned the holo signs. She wasn't looking for anything in particular, just taking it all in. Digesting the other worlds she knew so little about, doing her best *not* to think about Torin Kerridon and the revelation she'd unexpectedly shared with him.

Kala shook her head and let out another sigh. As surreal as Ati'aina was, it was not enough to stop her thinking of the damn *Sol* warrior.

What would be?

Nothing. Nothing would remove Torin from her mind. He was a part of who she was now. He'd turned her into a warrior and stolen her heart in the process. She was a walking weapon with one purpose. But she longed for another purpose—to belong to a man who believed her to be something she wasn't. Christ, could she be any more fucked up?

A high-pitched squeal rose over the cacophony of bustling pedestrians, fear ringing through its shrill note and Kala froze.

A small girl of four, maybe younger, pushed past her, her pale round face smudged with filth, her eyes wide with terror.

"Hey!" Kala called, turning after the child.

The little girl didn't stop, her tiny frame swallowed up straight away by the dense crowd.

"Where the fuck did the cunt go?"

The harsh snarl behind Kala made her turn and her gaze fell on a massive Andovian shoving his way through the pedestrians already scurrying out of his way. He cast the busy passageway a black scowl, baring jagged teeth, before glaring at an equally large Irithian beside him. "When I get my hands on the little piece of shit I'm going to fucking wring her neck to an inch of her worthless life."

"There!" his companion suddenly yelled, pointing frantically past Kala. "There! I see her!"

The Andovian's stare swung back to the bustling traffic behind Kala and his eyes erupted with brutal glee. "Yes. Got her."

Without thought or hesitation, Kala smashed her fist into his ugly, scaled face.

He reeled backward, arms pin-wheeling, head thrown back, his feet scrambling for balance. The Irithian beside him let out a loud shout and, expression both shocked and enraged, threw himself at Kala.

She spun, slamming her foot into his chest, sending him arcing backward. He landed with an *oof* amongst the gasping crowd, pain and stunned disbelief turning his face into an almost comical mask.

Kala didn't have time to laugh however. She ducked the Andovian lunging at her, punching him in the gut before sidestepping his wild blow.

"Fucking cunt!" he bellowed, swinging at her again. She dropped into a low crouch just as he snared a fistful of her hair. "I'm going to fucking tear you a—"

She threw herself into a tight, hands-free cartwheel, her abrupt momentum yanking him into a clumsy forward tumble. Her heel smacked into the side of his face and with a sharp yelp, his hand gripping her hair let go. She struck out again, slamming a back kick straight into his neck before spinning 180 degrees to drive her fist into the bellowing Irithian's chest— seconds before he could grab her from behind.

"You want to fuck little girls?" She fixed her stare on the Andovian where he stood hunched and wheezing, his eyes burning murderous rage. "How 'bout I fuck you up?"

He roared, leaping at her. She jumped out of his way, swinging her body into a spinning kick, her heel smashing into the base of his skull as he surged past her. There was a sharp crack, a sickening sound of bone shattering, and the Andovian fell face first to the floor.

Kala stared at his prone form, her blood roaring in her ears, her muscles burning with barely contained fury. "That's what you get, you sick bastard."

"Watch out!"

The shout from the crowd, loud and frantic, came too late. Something hit her in the temple. Hard. Something that felt like steel.

White agony erupted in the side of her head. Stole her sight. Her breath. She heard a gasp, followed by a sneering laugh, and then there was nothing.

Not even blackness.

Torin stood at the dark entryway of the last cubicle located in the most decrepit residential wing of Ati'aina, impatience gnawing at him like a ravenous beast. The old woman had commanded he wait, her violet eyes—so faded with age they were almost white—both stern and wary. Ignoring his growled protests, she'd slipped into the darkness without a backward glance, the stench of rotting meat hanging on the air in her absence like a thick cloud.

He let out a ragged sigh, suppressing the need to fidget. He had no doubt she would be watching him from within, gaining perverse pleasure from any harried agitation she perceived.

But if she doesn't come out soon, Kerridon, you're going in after her. You know that, don't you? Oracle of the Sol, *be damned, she will not make you wait much longer.*

Torin tightened his fists, the almost inaudible *pop pop* of his knuckles setting his teeth on edge. He didn't like this. He didn't like being treated like a child sent to the council elder. He liked being separated from Kala even less. The Old Seer had foretold the Oracle would not be cooperative in disclosing the Sun Sword's location and every second Torin waited at her door proved him correct once more.

"She is older than the known systems, Commander Kerridon," the Old Seer had told him more than two decades ago, a reverence in his voice Torin never believed possible. And a fear. "The first with the sight. The first to see the Immortals' weapon of life, the first to see its destructive force. If not for the Oracle, the *Sol* warriors would not be. She saw the first of the chosen *Sol*, those who gave their lives to procure the Sun Sword. She saw them and she commanded them."

Torin ground his teeth and glared into her residence. The Oracle had given birth to the *Sol* warriors, to their strength, and then a millennium later, destroyed them. All of them. Except Torin, who had been ordered by the Old Seer on a mission of seemingly little purpose or consequence to the distant planet of Tu. Torin knew that purpose now—to ensure his survival in the face of an undefeatable assault, an assault that left over a thousand *Sol* butchered, but knowing did not ease the pain and fury in his core. Nor the guilt.

He narrowed his eyes, those same emotions threading like thick ropes through his soul now. There was no known reason to the old woman's actions, no rationale to the word that had led to a mass execution, but by the five-hundredth year of her revelation, the Oracle had more followers, more zealots in her thrall, than all the old gods. When she'd declared the *Sol*'s time had come to an end, another five-hundred years later, the slaughter had begun.

The *Sol* had fought back, stunned by the betrayal of their creator, but their battle had not lasted long. How did they kill those they had trained their whole lives to protect?

Zealots however, fear nothing except the rejection and disapproval of their obsession and the Oracle had groomed those loyal to her to a frenzied point. The spilling of their own blood by the swords and disruptors of the *Sol* did not halt their lust to render the Oracle's words true. Within three solar months, the *Sol* were no more.

And with their demise, the Oracle had left the opulent temple in which she'd lived for over five centuries. Never to be seen or heard from again.

The Oracle will reveal the truth of the guard and the soul. The Oracle will reveal the light and the blade. The Oracle will reveal the truth of the fire and the flame. The Oracle will reveal the beginning and the end and her children will weep blood and drown in death.

The words of the *Sol* Edict were ingrained in Torin's existence. The old woman created the *Sol* Order, she'd discovered the Sun Sword, she'd seen the One Who Burns and the False Fire long before he, Torin Kerridon, command warrior and keeper of the Sun Sword's truth, had been born. The Oracle was the beginning and the end of his *Sol* brothers, and now here he was, on a spaceport so deep in space his ship's guidance system could not track the constellations, awaiting the insane woman's call.

If she did not tell him the location of the Sun Sword, he would be forced to demonstrate just how brutal the last of the *Sol* had become.

He shifted his feet, a prickle creeping up his spine. The seconds with Kala out of his sight were growing. He didn't like it.

"The *Sol* have always been impatient."

The raspy voice of the Oracle floated from the darkness and Torin stiffened.

"Eager to face their future. In a hurry to face their truth. It makes them what they are." A wild cackle bounced through the door, the sound both cold and unhinged. Torin curled his fists, the disquiet in his chest turning into a heavy knot.

"But never," the old woman's voice continued, "*never* have they been motivated by lust. Have you stuck your dick between the young thing's legs yet? Is she tight?" Another cackle, this one low and dirty. "Have you sampled her arse?"

Ice-hot fury flooded Torin's veins.

Fuck protocol.

He stormed into the Oracle's residence. How the old witch knew he was thinking of Kala didn't matter. Making her regret her words did.

Thick darkness folded around him, blinding him like a mask until, five steps in, his eyes adjusted and he found the Oracle's skinny frame bending over a large, metal container. "Watch your tongue, old woman," he growled, "before I remove it from your mouth."

She squealed, jolting upright and spinning to face him. "You are not allowed in here!" Eyes wide and rolling, she ran at him, waving something long and silver in her hand. "You cannot have it, you cannot have it! No! No! How dare—"

He snared her bony wrists, glaring down into her maniacal face. "Give me the Sun Sword, *Oracle*, and I will leave you alone."

She squirmed in his hold. "Let me go! By the *Sol* Edict, let me go!"

Torin growled. "You lost your right to invoke the *Sol* Edict the second you ordered the slaughter of my brother warriors." He dug his fingers harder into her wrists and jerked her closer, the stench of rotting meat seeping into his nostrils. "You destroyed the right to command *me* the second you spoke with such filth of Kala Rei."

"Kala Rei?" The old woman gasped. "The One Who Burns!" The blood drained from her face and she stilled, gaping up at him. "The One Who Burns is female?"

Something cold unfurled in Torin's gut. He stared at the Oracle, his muscles so tense he felt ready to snap. "The One Who Burns is female."

A sudden image flashed through his head. Kala wielding the Sun Sword. Sinking its burning blade into his neck.

His dream. His death. At Kala's hands.

False Fire.

He narrowed his eyes, yanking the old woman closer again.

"Give me the Sun Sword, Oracle. Now." He slid his gaze to the shiny length of light in her hand and let out a guttural curse.

Grasped in her gnarled fingers was a glow blade, a simple toy given to children to keep them entertained during long nights.

Syunna, she was insane.

He snapped his attention back to the old woman, lowering his head to glare straight into her bulging eyes. "Where. Is. The. Sword?"

The Oracle stared back at him, tugging on his grip. "Lemme go."

Torin suppressed the urge to shake her. Gone was the condescending seer. In her stead sulked a petulant child. "Where is the Sword?"

The old woman turned her head, tugging ineffectually against his grip again. "The Sun Sword is for the One Who Burns, not an honour-sick knight too dumb to realize his kind no longer exists."

Cold anger flowed through Torin. "This 'dumb knight" didn't turn his back on the prophecy when others did. This 'dumb knight' found the One Who Burns and trained her to be the supreme warrior she is. This 'dumb knight' knows just how precious she is." His chest tightened and he bit back a low growl. "To the worlds of man."

The Oracle stilled. She swung her stare back to his face, her sunken lips stretching into a wide smirk. "You are in *love* with her."

Torin shook her. He couldn't stop himself. "Tell me where the Sun Sword is, woman, before I lose my temper!"

The wild cackle filled the room again, gleeful and spiteful at once. *"The False Fire shall burn with the desire of the One and the One will fall to the Fire's flame. The lone warrior will perish to the forbidden lust and the hearts of man will perish to the One Who Burns."*

Torin's eyes widened and his breath stuck in his throat. "No."

The old woman grinned, nodding her head. "The Oracle never lies. You know that. It is ingrained in you. Everything you are was forged by me. My word is your life. Your existence is shaped by me." Her grin turned cruel. "Lone warrior."

"*Enough!*" Torin fixed the deceiving woman a level look, lowering his voice to a calm murmur. "Tell me where the Sun Sword is or by *my* word, *your* existence will be ended by *me*."

She shook her head, spiteful triumph burning in her eyes. And something else. Something cold dancing in the flames. "The One Who Burns," she hissed, hate in her words. "I must see the One Who Burns. Until Kala Rei stands before me the Sun Sword is beyond your reach." She lifted her chin, the room's dim light catching the hairs sprouting from it, making them appear like tiny spines. "And for every moment that is so, the worlds of man suffer more."

Torin felt his chest grow tight. He looked at the old woman. Knew her words to be true. Dread and apprehension rolled through him like a flooding river and he ground his teeth. He did not want to expose Kala to the Oracle's cruel insanity any more than he wanted to expose her to the old woman's cruel truth, but he had no choice.

It was Kala's destiny to wield the Sun Sword and he could not stop it being so.

Syrunna, how he hated that cursed weapon.

Throwing the Oracle's wrists away, he glared down into her face, the dim darkness of the room doing nothing to hide the maniacal grin she wore. "I will return with Kala Rei within the hour." He lowered his face closer to hers, letting her see the grim promise in his unwavering gaze. "If you are not here, I will hunt you down. If you are here with stupidity on your mind, I will kill you."

The old woman didn't say a word, but Torin saw her throat work in quick succession. He nodded. "Very good."

He turned and strode from the Oracle's cubicle, the putrid odor of decaying meat and unwashed flesh clinging to him like oily smoke. The bright lights outside the woman's residence attacked his eyes but he ignored the sting, heading for Ati'aina's central commercial levels. Pulling a small silver device from inside his jacket, he studied its tiny screen, biting back another curse. *Syunna*, Kala had explored the spaceport further than he anticipated. According to the small locator cuff he'd insisted she wear around her wrist, she was currently standing in Skin Strip, Ati'aina's notorious level dedicated to pleasure.

"By the gods, child," he growled, hurrying his step. "What are you doing there?"

He moved through the quiet residential corridors, a heavy pressure growing on his chest. Kala alone on the spaceport was bad enough. Kala alone on Skin Strip made his blood run cold.

You've trained her well, Kerridon. She can handle herself in any situation.

The assertion did nothing to ease his worry. To the contrary. He *knew* Kala. Barely six months ago she'd taken him on, a man almost double her size armed with a variety of very obvious weapons, with nothing more than a steel pipe and pure hatred. A horde of spiced-up, drunken smugglers and crooks would pose little threat to her thinking after half a solar cycle of intensive training.

"Fuck." Torin broke into a sprint, bursting from the quiet residential wing to shove his way through the crowded commercial levels.

Hawkers and vendors alike screeched their wares over the loud noise of the busy promenade, trying to outdo each other, trying to lure clients and customers into their establishments. The smells and sounds of each one assaulted Torin as he ran, sex, spice and liquor. His heart slammed against his breastbone, making his throat thick. What had he been thinking, letting Kala alone on such a place? Had he lost his mind?

No, just rational thought. But she took that from you the second she smashed you to the ground back on Earth.

He ground his teeth and ran faster, uncaring of the yells and shouts of protest he left in his wake. Skin Strip was but a few yards away, just around the next corner.

He took it without slowing down, searching the packed promenade for any signs of Kala.

Nothing.

Fuck.

He snatched a look at the locator device still clenched in his fingers. A tiny red point of light flashed directly to the right of where he stood.

He spun about, expecting to see her standing there.

She wasn't.

Lifting the locator device, he studied its display. His stomach rolled over. His pulse thumped in his neck. Something was wrong. Kala should be standing but a few feet away from him.

A numb tingle itched up his spine and he took a step forward, closer to the spot Kala should be. People pushed past him, their voices sliding off him, their presence forgotten. He moved closer to Kala's location. Closer. Closer.

Something silver glinted on the floor. Something small and circular. He sucked in a sharp breath, his mouth going dry. The locator cuff he'd slipped around Kala's wrist before they'd debarked *Helios Blade* lay on the metal floor, its locking clasp broken, its shiny surface stained red.

Blood.

Scanning the crowd moving around him, he grabbed a harried-looking Raavelian wearing a master-merchant's robes by the arm and jerked him to a halt. "Has there been an altercation here recently?"

The Raavelian tugged at Torin's grip, his eyebrows pulling into an irritated and somewhat apprehensive frown. "You're not port security. Let go of me."

Torin increased his pressure on the merchant's arm. "Answer my question."

The Raavelian's frown deepened, his expression growing more uncomfortable. "Some skinny girl picked a fight with an Andovian and an Irithian a few ticks ago."

A steady calm fell over Torin. His heart rate slowed, his breath grew even. "Did she win?"

The Raavelian snorted. "She was wiping the strip with them until the Ie'en turned up."

Torin held the merchant's stare. "What happened then?"

The Raavelian fidgeted, the skin around his nose pinching, an expression of sick disgust flickering across his face. "They took her."

Chapter Four

Kala remembered this feeling well—churning hate, cold fear, numb acknowledgement. She'd existed in this state her whole life. Until Torin had taken her from Earth, she'd known no other. Her stomach knotted but she shoved the physical reaction aside. It would not serve her any purpose in her current situation. She needed to focus.

"You're a tasty little thing," a raspy voice murmured in her left ear, sour hot breath licking at her flesh. A pointed claw pressed into the soft flesh under her chin, lifting and turning her head. She let her stare slide to the Ie'en, keeping her face emotionless. "Feisty, too." The Ie'en smirked, his black gaze skimming down the length of her body. "This will be fun."

Kala clenched her fists tighter but didn't fight against him or the Andovian standing behind her, his fingers curled around her biceps, holding her still. She gave the Ie'en a steady look. "Fun? You must have a different definition of the word from the one I know," she stated, pressing her feet more firmly to the steel floor. "Because quite frankly, anything involving you and me apart from me tearing your throat out is the furthest thing I can think of from fun."

The Ie'en laughed, crooked teeth glinting in the small room's dim light. Kala flicked a quick but thorough gaze over the confined space, inspecting everything within. To her left, behind the still pain-hunched Irithian, was a closed sliding door. On her right, one porthole showed the star-sprinkled blackness of deep space slowly sliding by. Various benches and surfaces jutted from the grimy walls, all clear of any objects. She refused to ponder the two chains hanging from the ceiling beside her head, both with unlocked shackles attached to their ends. But no matter how she much wished she could, there was no way to ignore the three idiots standing before her, one groaning lowly, one pressing his fat, hard dick to her backside, one leering into her face.

Her stomach knotted again, the familiar wave of hate and dread she thought she'd left behind growing stronger. What they intended to do to her was obvious. What she was going to do to stop them, not so much. Her gaze flicked to the shackled chains and her stomach tightened.

Think, Kala, think...

"I like a battle," the Ie'en stated, scraping his claw down her neck, over her collarbone to the V of her crudely mended vest. He hooked its tip under the stitched snakeskin and gave the item of clothing a little tug, his smirk spreading to a grin at the miniscule hint of extra cleavage the act revealed. "But I think with you, I will enjoy the show just as much." He turned his black gaze from Kala's chest to the Andovian behind her. "You can go first, Fruoc."

"Oi!" the Irithian protested. "Why does Fruoc get her first? I was the one who—"

"Let the scrunt slave you were chasing get away in the first place," the Ie'en finished, giving the Irithian a dark look. A chilly finger of fear traced up Kala's spine. Cruel intelligence shone in the Ie'en's black eyes. He reveled in pain, bathed in domination. She'd seen the same callous intellect in the eyes of the most brutal males back on Earth. It defined them. Elevated them above the pack mentality of their kind. The Ie'en wasn't just more intelligent than his two companions; he was more violent. Beating him in hand-to-hand combat wasn't going to be easy. If she lost...

Then don't lose.

Kala heard Torin's stern instruction murmur in her head. A heavy pulse beat in her neck at the remembered strength of his voice and she drew his face into her mind. He would be disgusted to see her in such a subjugated position. After the countless hours of training, of preparing her for the Sun Sword and her supposed fate, here she was, captured by three male slavers barely an hour after being on her own. Hot shame flooded through her.

"Chain her."

The Ie'en's sneered order snapped Kala's attention back to her three captors and she moved. Fast.

She threw herself backward, using the Andovian's massive body and cruel hold on her arms as a counter-pivot. She struck out with her feet, punching her heels into the Ie'en's gut, sending him tumbling over his own feet. He landed on his arse, but she didn't stop to enjoy the stunned rage igniting in his eyes. Slamming her feet to the ground, she tossed the Andovian over her shoulder. He came down with a resonating thud, his squeal of pain drowned out by the Ie'en's roar from the floor.

"Get her!"

The Irithian sprang at her, a level-one neutralizer in his fist, his expression both shocked and uncertain. His split-second hesitation served Kala well. She swung her right foot across her body, smashing her instep against his wrist. The neutralizer clattered from his grasp and he turned his head, following its path with his stare.

Kala spun, ramming her heel into his temple with a back

kick. A loud, wet crack filled the room and he went down—limp—bright green blood trickling from his nose and ear, white pus oozing from the ruptured mess of his eyeball.

"You've fucking killed him, you cunt!" the Andovian screeched behind her.

Kala snapped her head around just in time to see him leap at her. His claws swiped at her face, a wild insane grin turning his mouth into a toothy maw. She ducked, her heart thumping. Her palm itched for the feel of her training sword, its weight, its deadly blade. She'd be out of here already if she had it in her—

The Andovian came at her again. She struck out, slamming her right fist into his jaw, her left into his cheek. Bone shattered against her knuckles. The Andovian let out a high-pitched squeal. Kala shifted her balance, ready to kick him in the neck, and the Ie'en snapped up behind her and wrapped his arm under her chin.

The pressure hit her head instantly. The Ie'en flexed his muscles, the crook of his elbow jamming her head back, the hard steel of his biceps and forearm cutting the flow of blood to her brain. "Ten seconds, cunt, and you'll be unconscious. After that I could do anything I want to you and you wouldn't know."

Kala sank her nails into his arm, the pressure in her head growing. Blackness fogged the edges of her sight. Her lips began to tingle.

"But I don't want you unconscious," he went on, his breath painting her ear with hot moisture. "I want to see your eyes when I shove my dick into your cunt."

He jerked her back, hauling her feet from the floor, changing the position of his arm around her neck. Blood surged back through her veins, the sensation like acid pouring through her neck. She thrashed in the Ie'en's hold, her breath trapped in her constricted throat. Fuck, he was choking her.

The Andovian lumbered before her, blood seeping from the wound below his eye, his nose, the insane grin stretching his lips once more. Kala bucked, black splotches of oxygen-deprived pain blooming in her vision.

No. No. Oh, fuck, no!

Cold disgust rolled through her gut, sick panic gripping her chest. She knew what was going to happen next. Christ, how had she let it come to this?

No. Not again. Not again. Not this. Oh, God, no, not again.

She lashed out with her feet, her head fuzzy. Fogged.

"Now, I'm going to hold you just like this," the Ie'en murmured against her ear, his elbow around her neck squeezing tighter as he snaked his other hand over her hip, her belly, under the waistline of her trousers. His claw-tipped fingers pushed between her legs, at the folds of her sex. "And my colleague here is going to enjoy himself with this tight little cunt of yours." He released the choking pressure on her neck a little, coiling his arm tightly again before Kala could finish sucking in a breath. "And then," he went on, pulling her closer to his body with his delving fingers, "after he's had his fun, I'm going to fasten those shackles around your wrists and ankles and fuck you until there's no more come left in my dick." He pressed his lips to her cheek, holding her with his strangulating arm. "Do you understand?"

Kala stared at the grinning Andovian before her, the black splotches swarming over her sight, the Ie'en's fingers burrowing deeper between her legs. Her mind felt foggy, her limbs heavy. Cold fatality curled and flexed in the pit of her belly. This was happening. This was happening. All she needed was five seconds of freedom and her sword. All she needed was...all she needed was...

Torin.

Kala's head swam. Her heart stilled. She stared at the Andovian through the black splotches, unable to turn her head, unwilling to close her eyes.

Oh, God, no. Not this. Not this. Please, no.

The Andovian lurched closer to her, his hands fumbling with the release of his trousers, his eyes locked on hers. He grinned wider. "This is going to hurt, scrunt."

"Fuck you," Kala slurred, her brain shutting down.

"Yes," the Ie'en whispered. "That's the idea, isn't it?" He shoved his fingers harder into her sex, closing his arm tighter around her neck as the Andovian yanked his trousers open.

No. No. No, no no nononono

Blackness swarmed through Kala's head. She bucked once, the last of her oxygen spent, and felt the Andovian reach for her trousers. "Ready?"

"Yes," a deep, low voice growled. "Are you?"

Torin saw the Ie'en's black stare snap to him the second he spoke. Saw the slaver's thick, muscled arm jerk tightly under Kala's chin. Saw Kala's green-gold eyes roll back into her head and the cold calm that had enveloped him as he'd walked through Ati'aina tracking the three slavers who took her, cracked.

Syunna, Kala. Forgive me.

He stepped deeper into the small room—obviously a disused pay-as-you-go sex cubicle—the soft hiss of the door closing behind him like the breath of a night adder.

It was a good sound. A righteous sound. The sound of imminent death.

Their death.

The Andovian spun away from Kala, blood-orange eyes

snapping wide, the shock of seeing someone join their little soirée jolting him from his depraved intent. "Who the—"

"Kill the fucker!" the Ie'en spat, jerking Kala's limp body closer to his.

A detached fire ignited in Torin's soul.

By the Sun Sword's truth, he would make them suffer.

The Andovian leapt forward, his face distorting into a snarling mask, an illegal gutting blade suddenly in his hand.

Torin watched him come. And struck out.

He smashed his right heel into the Andovian's nose, his neck, his chest. The slaver reeled backward and Torin followed, pulling the knife from the Andovian's fist without slowing his stride. He swung his arm in a graceful curve, the short hooked blade slicing through the Andovian's jerkin into the soft flab of his belly with ease. Like a hot knife through jellied fat.

The Andovian squealed. He slapped his hands to the steaming ropes of gizzards spewing from his body, his eyes bulging. "*No!*"

Torin didn't pause. He moved like liquid, rote mechanics and elemental instincts guiding his hand upward in a tight arc, slicing the blade through the Andovian's throat and face in a deep, diagonal cut. The slaver squealed again, half his chin and jaw shearing off to dangle from his head on a glistening knot of sinew. Hot blood erupted from the cleaved wound, splattering Torin's face and chest and arm. And still he didn't stop. With another fluid arc, he brought the blade down and around, slicing its hooked length into the side of the Andovian's gushing neck, severing his head from his body.

Three cuts. Five seconds.

The Andovian slumped to the floor, the final, frantic beats of his heart pumping the last of his blood from his lifeless body, painting Torin's legs and boots with putrid ichor.

A sharp hiss turned Torin's head and he saw the Ie'en stumble backward, pulling Kala's limp body with him, his left hand still shoved between her thighs. "Holy fuck!"

Cold fury rolled through the detached fire burning in Torin's soul. "Let her go."

The Ie'en bared his teeth, an act Torin assumed was meant to be a show of threatening power. "Come any closer, fucker, and I'll fucking rip the cunt's throat open right now." His black eyes bulged. "Before you can save her, she'll be dead." His grip on Kala's neck coiled tighter and he stumbled back another step, heading for the closed door behind him. "Are you fast enough to stop me? Are you?"

Torin stared at the slaver. Serene bloodlust flowed over him. Through him. Turning the nothingness of his rage to an inferno. He gave the Ie'en a slow smile, welcoming the ravenous red haze. "Yes," he stated. "I am."

Kala scrunched her eyes, black pain throbbing though her head. She tried to move, but her body wouldn't listen. Cold. She was cold.

Why was she cold?

She fought to open her eyes, to lift her head from the cold beneath but the thick black pain fought against her.

Get up, damn it.

Her silent scream sent waves of anger through the agony in her head and she pressed her palms flat to the floor—*the floor? Why are you on the floor?*—forcing movement into her arms.

Something warm and sticky lapped at her fingers and she

drew in a shaky breath. The stench of blood and bile and piss filled her nostrils, poured into her body and she tried to open her eyes again. Blood? Whose blood? Whose piss? Why was she on the—

A scream tore through the air. High and deafening. Filled with absolute agony and terror—so wretched Kala's body and psyche jerked into action.

Her eyes snapped open, adrenaline surging through her veins. She blinked at the glistening liquid pooling around her, at the headless corpse of the Andovian beside her and the pit of her belly churned.

God, what the—

It all came back to her. In a flood of images and sensations. The little girl, the fight, the slavers, the Ie'en, his cruel fingers, the voice...

The scream came again, louder, higher, gurgling with liquid. She shoved herself upright, jerking her stare from the dead slaver to the wretched sound.

And her heart stopped.

Torin stood in the centre of the room, his massive body dripping blood and gore, his eyes blazing cold fire from an expressionless mask. His left hand knotted in a hank of the Ie'en's hair, holding him off the floor, his right hand buried wrist-deep in the screaming slaver's blood-gushing chest. "By the Sun Sword's truth." She heard him murmur the words, his voice like frozen gravel. "And for the One Who Burns."

His shoulder bunched, his nostrils flared and with one forceful, fluid jerk of his arm, he tore the Ie'en's heart from his body.

Kala slapped her hand to her mouth, stopping the gasp of horror before it could leave her throat. She stared at Torin, motionless, the dead Andovian's blood crusting on her flesh, the stink of piss and death stinging her nose. The *Sol* warrior stood as still as she, the Ie'en's heart in his hand, his eyes locked on the dead slaver's slack face.

He didn't move. He stood that way for endless seconds, as if a statue sculptured of some vengeful god. Kala watched him, her heart hammering, her mouth dry. She'd never seen him like this. It was terrifying. It was amazing. She wanted to go to him. She wanted to run from him—as far as she could.

What did she do?

She pulled breath after silent breath, staring at him. Her chest squeezed. For him. For her. God, what did she do?

His stare shifted, sliding to the heart in his fist. She saw his knuckles whiten, his forearm tense. Nothing happened for a split second and then the Ie'en's heart bulged and ruptured between Torin's fingers. "For the One Who Burns." He dropped the crushed organ to the floor, pain etching each whispered word. His eyes closed and with a low growl, he released his grip on the slaver's matted hair.

The corpse fell to the blood-soaked floor with a wet thud.

Kala swallowed, her stare locked on Torin's profile.

He studied the lifeless mess at his feet, his jaw clenched, his shoulders bunched. Icy energy radiated from him in chilling waves, made all the more ominous by the soft sound of the Ie'en's blood dripping from his right hand—a repetitive beat that seemed to crack the oppressive silence of the room and tear at Kala's nerves.

She didn't move.

"We have to go," he suddenly said, still staring at the Ie'en's body, the torment in his voice gone. Shoulders straightening, he turned his head and looked at her, his eyes expressionless. "There is someone who must see you."

Kala's stomach twisted. She swallowed, studying Torin where he stood, uncertain how to react. "Who?"

He stepped toward her, an unreadable light flickering in his eyes. "There are things that need to be said, Kala." His voice sounded flat, devoid of any life. "Things that need to be done, but we don't have the time now." He turned his head away, casting a long look at the carnage around them, his face still carved from granite. "I am sorry, but we have to go."

He turned and crossed the small room, stepping over the Ie'en's corpse as he headed to the closed door. Without looking over his shoulder to see if she followed, he activated the opening mechanism and stepped out into the corridor.

A cold fist reached into Kala's chest and squeezed her heart. She closed her eyes for a quick moment before climbing to her feet. She'd been violated. Attacked. She was still foggy from the slavers' assault on her and it all meant little compared to the ache threatening to overwhelm her at the sight of Torin's tense back.

What did you expect him to do, Kala? Come to you? Take you in his arms?

She closed her eyes again and shook her head. No. But she wished he had.

There are things that need to be said, things that need to be done.

His emotionless words echoed in her mind and she ground her teeth. His behavior unnerved her. Confused her. He should be yelling at her by now. Berating her for her failure. Demanding she drop to the floor and give him one hundred pushups as punishment for her inadequacies. Why wasn't he admonishing her for getting caught? For being beaten? Was he doubting her? Damning her? Swallowing the thick lump in her still-sore throat, her head throbbing, her body aching, she stepped over the dead Ie'en and followed her mentor.

He moved through the spaceport's passageways with determined speed, ignoring the gasps and shocked cries of those he stormed past. Kala was not surprised by their reaction. The black leathers he wore glistened with blood, his skin painted by it in streaming tendrils. He looked beyond menacing. He looked demonic.

Fighting the cold disquiet gnawing at her, she hurried to keep up. His silence unnerved her and yet, at the same time, the parting wave of the crowd before them sent a perverse sense of pride deep into her being.

He *was* a man to fear. Not just because of his physical size and prowess, but because of his presence. He was undeniable. His honour was unlike any she'd experienced, unbending and unassailable. His strength and belief was unlike any she'd known, invincible and intimidating. He would do anything to protect those needing protection in the name of the *Sol* Edict and the Sun Sword. He would give his life if needed—of that she had no doubt. It was easy to see why she loved—

She came to an abrupt halt and stared at his back. "Oh, no." She shook her head, her heart leaping into rapid flight. "No."

She couldn't be in love with him.

Why not? You've just listed every reason why you are.

Her throat squeezed tight and she closed her eyes. That he was sexually attracted to her was undeniable. She'd seen it in his eyes, felt it in his body. Heard it in his words—*I want you, Kala. So fucking much*—but who *was* she?

An acrid chill slithered through her. Someone he needed to save when she shouldn't need saving, that was who. Someone to be defended when she shouldn't be defenseless. He was every woman's fantasy—a hero, a rescuer, a man of smoldering passion and incomparable strength, and she was not worthy of him. She was damaged goods. Soiled by a life she'd never wanted. After six months of being molded by him, trained by him, forged to become the savior of the worlds of man, she was nothing he believed her to be.

She opened her eyes and continued after him, the ache in her heart, her core, growing, her body numb. What did she do now?

"Here." Torin's blunt growl startled her out of her bleak reverie. He stopped at the end of a dank corridor before an open doorway, every muscle in his body tense. His stare fixed on the black opening. He stood motionless, yet Kala sensed that same icy energy from the sex cubicle thrumming through him still. He appeared on edge, ready to...what? Attack?

"Who is in here?" A cold pressure curled around Kala's heart. She had no idea what was going on, but she didn't want to be here. Something felt wrong. Her skin prickled and she looked over her shoulder, convinced someone watched her. She could almost feel their heavy stare crawling over her like a physical touch she wanted no part of. The corridor stood empty behind her, its darkened length curling away from where she stood, devouring the weak yellow light. Turning back to Torin, she frowned. "What's going on?"

Torin kept his stare locked on the doorway. "The Oracle is inside." Contempt turned the statement to a low snarl. "She has information I need. She will not give it to me until she sees you."

Kala narrowed her eyes, the pressure on her chest, the prickle on her flesh growing more intense. "Because I am the One Who Burns?"

His jaw bunched. "Because you are the One Who Burns."

A chill rippled up her spine and she suppressed the need to

fidget. "And who is she, to be so curious?"

Torin's nostrils flared. "She is the beginning and the end of the *Sol.*"

The statement turned the chill tracing her spine to a scalding burn. Kala studied his profile. What did that mean? The beginning and the end of the *Sol?* And why did he say it with such empty contempt? She frowned, wishing more than anything she could reach out and place her palm to the side of his face. Cup his jaw. Brush the pad of her thumb over his lips and tell him it was okay. But she didn't know if it was. And she didn't know if he would stay her hand. So instead, she released a sigh and peered into the darkness beyond the doorway. "So what? Is she just going to pop out her head and take a look at me? Should I show her my teeth?"

Torin turned his head, his eyes burning with a disgust Kala felt in the pit of her belly. "She is dangerous," he stated. "But I will protect you. Do not be afraid."

The statement struck Kala like a cold punch. Protect. Afraid. Words Torin had not uttered to her since the second day of her training. She lifted her chin. "I do not need to be protected." She glared at the dark opening before her. "And I am not afraid. Let her do her worst."

A rising cackle followed her words, a putrid, overwhelming stench of rotting flesh rolling out of the black cubicle. "My worst is far more heinous than the *Sol* warrior would ever let you know, child," a raspy female's voice chuckled from within. "But it is not for you to fear." A short, hunched woman shuffled from the darkness, stepping from its thick curtain like an apparition. Her pale violet stare fixed on Kala's face, a toothy smile stretching flaky lips as she drew closer. "At least, not yet."

Kala stiffened, doing everything she could not to cover her nose and mouth with her hand. She stared down at the wizened old woman, the sight of three gutted rabbit carcasses hanging from her neck almost making her gag.

"So." Stroking the flickering glow stick she grasped in her bony hands, the hag looked Kala up and down, a brazen inspection that filled her mouth with bile. "You are the One Who Burns." She gave Torin a quick smirk. "I see why you want to stick your dick between her legs, *Sol*. I bet she is tight and—"

"Another word, Oracle," Torin growled, his stony expression never changing, "and you will lose your tongue."

Kala's stomach rolled. At the old woman's words and Torin's.

The Oracle shifted on her feet, shimmying away from him, giving Kala a wide smile as she did so. "Do you dream of him, child?" She nodded towards the motionless warrior. "Tell ol' Marl what you long for him to do to you."

Abruptly, as if commanded into existence by an unseen force, a vivid image of Torin flashed through Kala's head: his naked body slicked in sweat, his hips aligned with hers, his lips on her breasts. Her sex constricted, gripping a cock that wasn't there, longing for a fulfillment denied her. She narrowed her eyes, glaring at the old woman. "That's none of your—"

"Oooh, such a dirty mind for one so young," the hag cut her off, wrinkled hands slapping together, the glow blade clanking against the multitude of silver rings hanging loosely around each bony finger. "You are growing more interesting by the second."

Kala clenched her fists, the bile in her mouth growing more bitter. She straightened her spine, drawing herself as tall as she could be. "I am the One Who Burns, Oracle. Tell me what I need to know so I can be done with you."

The old woman's eyebrows shot up. "The One Who Burns! The One Who Burns!" She cackled with apparent glee, pocketing the glow blade in the voluminous fold of her filthy gown. Swiping at the rabbit carcasses, she shuffled a step closer, her pale eyes a sick puce in the dim yellow light. "I will be the one who decides that, child."

With blurring hands, she snared Kala's wrist and yanked her downward, licking her face from chin to eye in a single stroke. "You taste like the *Sol*," she declared with a grin, releasing Kala as quickly as she'd grabbed her. "Has he tasted you yet?"

"That's enough, Marl."

Kala jerked her stare from the old woman to Torin's stormy face, her pulse pounding in her throat so hard she could barely draw breath. God, who *was* this woman?

"You want answers, Torin Kerridon," the hag rasped, "then leave us. The child and I have things to discuss." She flashed him a smile, the putrid odor of decaying teeth oozing from her mouth. The old woman turned back to Kala, bestowing her with a wider smile. "*Womanly* things," she went on.

Torin's jaw bunched and cold fury flared in his eyes, the first emotion Kala had seen from him since she'd regained consciousness on the floor.

"I will not leave her alone with you."

Bulging eyes shone with malicious glee. "You have no choice."

Kala turned to Torin. She gave him a level look, a hot pressure behind her eyes. He would not leave her, not unless she told him to do so, and until he did... "Leave us, keeper of the Sun Sword's truth. I am in no need of your presence."

He hissed in a sharp breath, his whole body stiffening as his stare locked on hers. He didn't move, and once again Kala felt her skin awash in a million pinpricks of hot needles. She parted her lips to order Torin away, but before she could do so he turned and strode down the corridor.

Kala's chest squeezed and she bit back the shout on her lips. She didn't want to be alone with this woman. She wanted Torin to leave her even less.

God, what was she doing?

"Exactly what you have to do, child," the old woman whispered, leaning closer. "To protect the man you love from what he doesn't need to hear."

Kala's heart leapt into her throat, her mouth turning dry. "And what's that?"

The Oracle's withered lips stretched into a wide grin. "That you are going to kill him."

Zroya lifted his head from the metal floor of his quarters and looked at the object before him, the low hum of his ship's engines sending vibrations through his legs up into his already tight balls.

He studied the long blade hovering mere inches above the floor, its impossible, unbreakable length aglow with golden fire.

He had felt the Immortal's weapon call to him the moment he could form cognitive thought, an undeniable longing in the pit of his belly for something more, something his ineffectual child's mind couldn't understand. It wasn't until his master found him, beaten and abused and starving that the longing was given a name—destiny.

The prophet spoke to him at great length of the weapon, of how the Immortals forged it from their force. How they created it to right the worlds of man, punish them for their insolence and heathen savagery. How the Youngest had created the seed and the Eldest, the perversion. He devoured each raspy word, letting each one slip into his ear and become a part of his soul. His master told him the old gods had created the weapon to be wielded by a warrior of incomparable might, a warrior who would mark the worlds of man as his own and rule them with merciless strength. A warrior who burned with all the pain of a primitive species and all the hate of a brutalized child.

Zroya gazed at the Sun Sword. *He* was that warrior. His master told him so every day. It was his destiny. Every day for the last twenty-seven solar years the prophet had consulted the Immortals through the blood of the female animals he wore around his waist. When the old gods spoke with ambiguity, his master would seek the answers through the blood of the female humans he ordered Zroya to slay. With every kill, his master spoke more fiercely of the One Who Burns until nothing mattered to Zroya but possessing the weapon and enslaving the female cunt who dared believe that weapon to be hers.

Zroya smiled. His utter and complete domination and control of the worlds of man would begin with the utter and complete domination and control of the False Fire.

Something tight and hot twisted in his groin and he groaned, hungering for the cunt almost as much as he hungered for the burning blade before him.

He stared at it harder, craving its weight in his hands. What made the Sun Sword burn no one knew. His master told him it was the smoldering heart of the centre of the universes that gave it light. Zroya didn't care. With the Sun Sword in his hands *he* would be the centre of the universes, not some mystical burning ball of energy.

Twenty-seven years he'd prepared. Twenty-seven years of training—from one instructor to another, from one planet to the next—and once he had learned all he could from each, once his master had deemed his training in each weapon and fighting style complete, he'd slaughtered his instructor and moved to the next. Growing closer to being the perfect weapon. Closer to being ready to claim what was his to claim. Until the day had come when the prophet had told him it was time to hunt the False Fire.

Destiny.

His groin grew heavier at the intoxicating thought and he straightened from his prostrate position, his gaze still focused on the iridescent sword. Soon the False Fire would be his. Soon the Immortal's blade would be his, and with it the worlds of man would be his.

A kaleidoscope of incandescent colour rippled through the glorious weapon before him and his master limped through the hologram, turning it into a distorted image of fractured light. The prophet came to a halt, the sword shimmering back to perfection behind him. "As revealed in the blood of the mistaken," he spoke, his voice less scratchy than normal, "the False Fire has met with the Oracle."

Zroya snapped to his feet, his heartbeat doubling. "And?"

His master's white gaze slid to him. "And the false one shall be in your possession within the day's half cycle." His thin lips curled into an emotionless smile and he stroked one gutted rabbit corpse hanging from his belt. "Are you ready, my child?"

Zroya's dick flooded with eager blood. His palms itched with lust. His mouth filled with saliva. "Yes, my master." He bowed, his stare returning to the holographic Sun Sword glowing behind the old man. "I am ready."

Chapter Five

The soft sound of Kala's steady footfalls alerted Torin to her approach. He pulled in a slow breath and stood motionless, forcing away the irritation scouring at his nerves as he watched the dark passageway for her arrival.

She rounded the corner, her expression set in an unreadable mask. Anger squeezed Torin's throat tight and he bit back a sharp curse. The Oracle had said something to upset her.

Two steps away from him, Kala stopped, the shadows of the corridor playing over her face. "The old woman wants to speak with you."

Her voice was short, clipped. Torin ground his teeth. He studied Kala, wanting nothing more than to take her hand and pull her to his body, smoothing her hair as he pressed his lips to the top of his head, her temples. Kissing away her pain. Wanting to show her how sorry he was for what she'd experienced since boarding Ati'aina, everything she'd suffered since he'd entered her life. Instead, he gave her a curt nod. "Return to *Helios Blade*. This will not take long."

The skin around Kala's eyes pinched as she fought to control whatever emotion his order evoked in her. Self-contempt rolled through him, turning the saliva in his mouth to sour bile, but he ignored it. The Oracle had seen the One Who Burns. He,

Torin, had met his end of the agreement. Now the old crone must meet hers.

Fixing his stare on the dark passageway leading to the Oracle's cubicle, he moved past Kala. A hot prickle across his shoulders told him she was studying him, watching him walk away from her, as if her gaze had ignited the sun tattooed on his back into real flames. Syunna, how he wanted to turn around. To see what emotion burned in her eyes.

He curled his fists and continued along the empty corridor. It was of no consequence. What he longed for could never be. She was not his to have and all he brought to her was pain and heartache. It would be best if Kala hated him.

"She is a pretty young thing, *Sol.*" The raspy voice scraped over his senses and he drew his focus onto the old woman standing at her cubicle door. "I can see why you desire her."

Torin clenched his jaw. "Tell me the location of the sword, woman, so I can be done with you."

The Oracle raised her eyebrows, her pale eyes gleaming in the muted light. "The 'sword'? The '*sword*'? Is that bitter contempt I hear in your voice, Torin Kerridon? Where is the reverence? The respect?"

He leveled his stare on her face. "The location, before I lose what little control I still have."

A flicker of something dark crossed the old woman's eyes and she shuffled back a few steps, the hand gripping the glow blade rising to her chest.

Torin suppressed a bleak smile. Finally, she was scared of him. Good.

The old woman's eyelids fluttered, once, twice and she looked up at him, a clouded veil fogging her gaze. "The sword that will save the hearts of man smolders in the heart of the two moons with one soul," she intoned. "The sword that will pierce

100

the heart of the last warrior will be found in the one soul. The sword that will—"

Torin snatched the Oracle's wrist in his fist and jerked her towards him, cold rage threatening to undo him. "Cut the shit, Marl."

The old woman trembled, eyes wide and clear once more. "The Sun Sword is on the second inner moon of P'Helios," she blurted in a hurried whisper. "In the forgotten *Sol* Temple. Look for the sun and the heart and the weapon will be beneath. Only the One Who Burns or the False Fire may release it from its prison."

A sharp sense of completion rolled through Torin, bringing with it numb emptiness. He released his grip on the Oracle's wrist and stepped back. "If you lie..."

The old woman shook her head, face growing frantic. "I do not lie, *Sol*. I do not lie. The Sun Sword is where I have spoke. It is the very place I severed the life cord that bound you to your mother. Her blood and the blood of your birth still stains the sacred altar."

Torin narrowed his eyes. "My blood?"

"Your blood, Torin Kerridon. I knew of you a century before I knew of the One Who Burns. I awaited your birth just as much as the stars did." The Oracle cowered lower, her shoulders hunching as if the weight of his stare was too much to bear. "Now be gone," she whimpered, clutching the glow blade tighter to her breast. "You taint the air with the death that surrounds you."

Her words sliced into Torin, made him cold, hot. Questions bubbled up through the shock consuming him, but he denied them. They were of no importance. He was just one fallen warrior charged with a task almost complete.

He turned from the sniveling old woman and began

walking. He had the location of the sword. He had the one destined to wield it. As soon as he brought the two together his role in this whole fucked-up prophecy was over.

"No, Torin Kerridon!" The Oracle's screech rose behind him. "You're wrong. Your blood feeds the death of the heart and only your blood will nourish the heart's savior!"

He shut the old woman's insane cries from his head, rounded the bend and headed for his ship. There was work to be done. There were preparations to be made. And when it was over and he would wipe his hands of Kala, the Sun Sword, the whole insane farce. Regardless of what the Oracle insisted.

Regardless of what his heart desired.

Helios Blade sat silent as he crossed its entry hatch, a sleeping deep-space craft capable of phenomenal speed and power. He'd spent most of the last solar cycle within its form, and never had it felt like a punishment until now. Now, it was an inescapable reminder of everything he was and everything he could not ever be.

He moved through its belly, stripping his jacket from his body as he did so. The leather clung to him, already growing stiff with drying blood, and he threw it aside with disgust. It had been a long time since he'd been so coldly violent in his actions. The Ie'en's blood crusting on his clothes, his flesh, only served to highlight how ruthless and vicious he could be. After decades of the Old Seer's calm guidance, he'd thought he'd left the savage brutality of the *Sol*'s training behind. But then he'd seen Kala in the Ie'en's vile embrace, the bastard's hand stabbing between her legs, the Andovian looming over her, his dick in his hand, and it all came back to him—the bloodlust, the icy fire in the pit of his belly devouring his control, his humanity. The instinctual calling for ruthless pain that had elevated him to command warrior status before he'd even grown hair on his jaw.

Torin raked his fingers through his hair, the Oracle's words taunting him: *You taint the air with the death that surrounds you.*

He quickened his pace, denying the ache in his soul. He had no time for self-pity. He had to get to P'Helios. He had to get Kala to the...

He faltered to a halt and closed his eyes.

Syunna, at the mere thought of her his body erupted in yearning heat. Every molecule, every fibre in his being strained for her, no matter how much he willed it otherwise. He could feel her very presence on his ship, a source of life and energy that called him with more potency than all the need for bloody revenge. He didn't need to check the internal bio-scans to know she was in the training room. He could feel her there, waiting for him.

Go to her.

He ground his teeth and shook his head.

Go to her. Tell her.

Tell her what? That the reason for her existence was about to come to pass? That the life of every living being in every universe awaited her?

That you are sorry. For everything. That you love her.

Torin bit back a curse and began storming toward the cockpit. He would not tell her that. P'helios' second moon was two hyper clicks away. The fate of the future hung in the balance. Like it or not, he was the last of the *Sol*, the keeper of the Sun Sword's truth, a warrior created to do one thing and one thing only and he had work to do.

Numb resolution squeezing his chest, he stepped into the cockpit.

And found Kala standing there. Looking at him.

His gut knotted. "I thought you were in the training room."

"I was."

He stared at her, the pulse in his neck rapid. At some point since leaving him on Ati'aina she had showered and the clean scent of her skin filled his every breath. His nostrils flared and a low groan caught in his throat.

She swallowed, her eyes unreadable. "You are angry."

Torin's pulse quickened. "Yes."

Kala nodded. Once. "With me."

"No."

The word passed Torin's lips in a blunt growl. He turned his head to the side. Stared at the stars beyond *Helios Blade*'s viewscreens. He could feel her. Feel her breath heat the air, feel her heartbeat disturb the cosmos. By the gods, why could he feel her so powerfully when he could not have her? Why did he—

"Make love to me."

Kala's soft command snapped his stare back to her face.

"Make love to me, Torin," she said again, just as soft, just as commanding.

He shook his head. "You don't know what—"

"Yes," she cut him off, taking a step toward him. "I do." She took another step, her heat reaching for him. "I know what I'm saying. I know what I'm doing." She stopped before him, her thighs brushing his, her palms pressed to his bare chest. "I want you to make love to me until time ceases to exist."

A wave of something elemental and undeniable rolled through Torin. His throat grew thick, his flesh grew hot. He looked down into Kala's face. Saw a future forever beyond his reach in her eyes. Saw her desire. Saw her pain.

He saw it all and wrapped his arms around her body. Drew her closer still, until there was nothing between them, not even the shadow of their destined paths, and kissed her.

She kissed him back. Unreservedly and completely. Her lips parted and her tongue slipped into his mouth, tangling with his, mating with it. Torin groaned, fisting the snakeskin of her vest at the small of her back and pulling her harder to his body. He tasted her mouth, her tongue, nipped at the soft fullness of her bottom lip, flicked at the smooth evenness of her teeth. She whimpered in reply and slid her hands up to his shoulders, curled her arms around his head. Her fingers buried in his hair, pulling his head down. He felt her body tremble, felt her nipples pinch hard against his chest.

He groaned again. She was so small, so tiny. Perfection and furious strength all at once. He could break her with his two hands and she could break him with her lips.

Raw pleasure surged through his body at the giddy thought. He dragged his mouth from hers, scored a line of kisses down the bowed column of her throat, back up to her chin, her jaw, her lips again.

She traced the edges of his mouth with her tongue, slow strokes that harbored no hesitation or doubt. Another tremble claimed her and he felt her rise up onto the tips of her toes, her hands turning to tight fists in his hair, her body pressing harder to his.

With a harsh groan, Torin tore his mouth from hers, scooped his arms under her legs, her back, and lifted her from the floor.

She gasped and he caught the sound with his kiss, holding her to his chest as he strode from the cockpit. *Helios Blade*'s corridors and passageways were ingrained into his psyche and he moved through his ship without the need for sight. Kala curled in his arms, her heat mingling with his, the taste of her lips teasing his thirst.

He wanted all of her. He wanted to taste every inch of her body, her soul.

Cool air blew against his hot flesh as he crossed the training room's threshold, rippling his arms and legs with a delicious chill. His nipples pinched hard and he moaned, louder again as Kala slipped one hand from his hair to his chest, capturing the puckered tip of flesh between her fingertips.

Gods, yes.

The silent cry echoed through Torin's mind and he came to a halt, knowing exactly where they stood in the large area without needing to tear his lips from Kala's. He dropped to his knees on the central mat, its cushioned expanse taking his weight, redistributing its impact. Muscles straining, not from exertion but from mounting pleasure, he gently lowered her to the floor—bottom first, then legs, back and shoulders. He slid his arms from beneath her, moving his lips over hers, touching her teeth with the tip of his tongue as her head came to rest on the floor.

She played her fingers over his hard nipple, gripped the hair at his nape with fierce strength as he rose above her, over her. He placed one leg over her thighs, his cock so hard hot pain speared into his balls and the pit of his stomach. She shifted beneath him, aligning her hips with his, her tongue delving into his mouth with hungry urgency.

He could feel the energy of her desire thrumming through her body. It called to his, charging him. His blood seemed to surge through his veins like liquid fire. He pressed his palms to the floor on either side of her head, keeping his torso from touching her body. If he were to experience the sensation of her breasts crushing against his chest now control would be lost. He wanted to claim her. Fuck, he wanted to not just *claim* her, but take her. Possess her. Despite the scalding urgency of his desire her words from a lifetime ago haunted him—*the men would always find me.* His chest squeezed with a gripping pressure and he skimmed one hand over her jawline in a gentle caress. She'd experienced so much horror. *Her* pleasure was what mattered. Not his. She had given him this moment and he would give her everything she'd never had. True pleasure in physical connection. True connection in physical pleasure.

Even if it drove him mad fighting his own longing need.

He stoked her inner thigh with his knee, nudging her legs apart. The air filled with the delicate musk of her sex and Torin's head swam. He wanted to lift his head and gaze into her eyes, but feared the loss of her lips against his.

A soft moan sounded in her throat and she moved beneath him, parting her legs farther. He took his weight further on his hands and arms, pressing his knee to the junction of her thighs, rubbing it slowly against the curved mound of her sex.

She moaned again, louder, stronger and this time Torin could no longer deny the need to see her face, to see the pleasure in her eyes. He tore his mouth from the kiss and gazed down at her, his heart slamming against his breastbone, his breath ragged in his chest.

He should not have done so. The sight of her obvious rapture—parted lips, half-lidded eyes, flushed cheeks—was too much. He growled, his cock flooding with scalding desire, and took her mouth again.

She met his hunger, thrusting her hips from the floor to

grind her softness to his knee, her tongue fighting with his as she did so, conquering, surrendering, willing. Her hands stole to his shoulders, tugged on them. He resisted her, knowing he was not strong enough to withstand the touch of her body completely under his. There was so much more he wanted to do before he surrendered to his own release. So much he wanted to make her feel.

Dragging his mouth from her lips, he charted a languid course along her jaw, down her neck. She hitched in a shallow breath and sank her nails into his shoulders, pushing her sex harder to his knee. "Please..."

Her plea sent a ripple of something primitive through Torin. "Kala." His voice was as ragged as his breath. "I want to take this slow for you. I want to show you how pleasurable—"

She shook her head. "I don't want slow, Torin." She lifted one leg and wrapped it around his thigh, drawing his knee harder to her heat. "I've had six months of slow. Every moment I've been with you has been building to this." She arched her back, her eyes closing as she ground her groin to his knee again. "Please."

Torin closed his own eyes, drawing a deep breath into his lungs. The need to tear his trousers from his body, tear Kala's from hers and sink his hard, aching cock into her sex surged through him. His shoulders bunched, ready to propel him into an upright position to do just so, but he stayed as he was, partially suspended above her by the coiled muscles of his arms and the tenuous strength of his willpower. The vivid memory of Kala's last orgasm, the fear in her eyes, the terror in her voice, haunted him with too much power. He had to fight his desire.

Syunna, are you really that strong?

A hot ball welled in his chest. For Kala, he would be.

He gazed down at her. Gave her a small smile. "Trust me,

Kala Rei." He lowered his lips to her mouth and placed the softest of kisses there. "I will show you what it means to be the One Who Burns."

He slid his knee from between her legs, his smile turning to a grin at Kala's whimpered protest. Ignoring her attempts to pull him down to her body, he pressed his mouth to her throat, her collarbone. Maneuvering his weight onto one hand, he released the front clasps of her vest, parting the snakeskin garment with a gentle nudging of his fingers until it slid open, revealing her breasts to his caress. He scooped one up, worshipped its perfection with his hand, his fingers. Kala gasped, the sound followed by a hitching moan as he rolled his thumb over her nipple.

The tip of flesh puckered instantly into a rock-hard nub and liquid heat pooled in Torin's groin. He suppressed a growl, dropping his head instead to take the pinched nipple in his mouth, flicking his tongue over it, nipping it with his teeth before suckling on it with gentle force.

"God!" Kala burst out, her nails raking at his back.

He drew her nipple deeper into his mouth, sucked harder. She whimpered again, her hips bucking from the floor, her hands gripping his back.

Torin's head swam. His cock pulsed. With more control than he thought he possessed, he dragged his mouth from her breast, rained a slew of tiny kisses over the slight plane of her chest and then captured her other nipple with his lips.

Kala cried out, a tremble in her voice and body. "That feels...that feels..." The rest of her words became lost in another moaning cry. Torin suckled harder, nipping with increasing pressure. She writhed beneath him, her hands scratching at his back, his shoulders. "Please, Torin." She tangled her fingers in his hair and tugged. "Please. I want to feel you inside me."

Lifting his head, Torin pulled a steadying breath through his nose. "True pleasure comes from giving, Kala, just as much as taking." He let his gaze roam over the sight of her flushed breasts, the glistening sheen of his saliva on her right nipple almost pushing him over the edge. "I have longed to do this for a lifetime."

Her eyes fluttered closed and a soft choke caught in her throat. "But I can't wait any longer."

A smile pulled at Torin's lips and he smoothed his hand down to her belly, skimming his fingers under the waistline of her trousers. "Tell me this doesn't feel as good as you want it to feel and I will stop. I will move right on and bury my cock to the balls between your legs."

Kala's stomach dipped, her hitching breath and lifting hips heating his already molten blood. "Yes...no..." She opened her eyes, rolled her head to the side, pushed her hips higher to his touch. "I..."

Torin lowered his head to her stomach, pressed his lips to the flat perfection just below her navel. "Let the pleasure take you, Kala." He touched the tip of his tongue to her flushed skin. "Let it consume you."

"Oh, God."

Her groan rumbled through her belly. Torin felt it with his lips. It fueled his own pleasure. With every breath he took, he could smell her juices growing wetter between her legs. She was more than ready for him to fill her, more than ready to have him bury his length into her creamy heat, and yet he knew she could feel more. Knew he could give her more.

With a quick flick of his fingers, he opened her fly, marking the newly revealed flesh with his mouth as he smoothed her trousers down her hips and arse. Kala moaned, her hands dropping from his hair to scramble at the mat beside her. She knew what was coming next. The fresh musk scenting the air told Torin as such.

Lifting his head slightly, he watched his fingers feather over the glistening folds of her sex, watched them circle the tiny nub of her clitoris. A surge of tension flooded his groin, turned his straining cock into a throbbing shaft of want, but he held onto his control. "I am going to taste you now, Kala." He sucked in a slow breath through his nose, his stare fixed on her cream-sodden pussy. "I am going to make love to you with my mouth, bring you to climax with my tongue." He stroked her damp folds with his fingertips, marveling at her velvet beauty. "And then, as you ride each peaking wave of pleasure, I am going to break my solemn word I gave six months past and sink my cock into your heat and take you even higher still."

Kala's choked whimper caressed his ears as he lowered his head to the junction of her thighs and delved into her pussy with his tongue.

"Oh, God!" Kala cried, her hips bucking upward, slamming her sex to his face. "God, God!"

Torin plunged his tongue past the drenched lips of her pussy, stabbing into her tightness. She tasted just as he knew she would—salted honey and musk. He could drown in her flavor and it would be a good death. He licked at her clit, flicked its swollen form with the tip of his tongue, sucked it into his mouth and nipped it with his teeth.

Kala cried out, her hands grasping at the mat, her hips jerking in thrusting jolts. Her juices flowed from her sex, wetting Torin's chin. He drank in her pleasure, smoothing his hands over her legs, the firm strength of her inner thighs adding to the exquisite sensations flooding through him. Everything in his life had led to this moment. Everything. The Sun Sword, the *Sol* Order, the prophesies, all insignificant to this one stolen moment of shared pleasure.

His body ached, thrummed with a building tension he knew he would not be able to constrain for much longer. Rational thought began to escape him.

Rolling his tongue over Kala's clit, he curled his hands under her arse, cupping her cheeks with a pressure he hoped was gentle but knew to be not. Slipping. He was slipping.

Syunna, she tastes so good...so good...

He plunged his tongue back into her folds, wriggled its length deeper. Kala bucked again, her moans growing faster, shorter. With a quick tug, he jerked her hips higher and pressed his mouth to the tight hole of her anus, stabbing at the puckered entry with the tip of his tongue as he dipped one finger, two, three into her pussy. Kala's moans turned to gasping cries. Her sex squeezed his fingers, warm cream slicking his knuckles as she bucked into his penetrations.

"Oh, Torin, Torin." His name fell from her lips in breathless pants. She thrust harder into his hand. He wriggled his fingers, stroked the sweet spot within her sex and then replaced his hand with his mouth again, lapping at the wet product of his touch.

"I'm going to...I'm going to..."

He closed his lips tightly on her clit, sucked hard. Flicked the tip of his tongue over the tiny button, before plunging his tongue into her centre once again.

"God, Torin!" Kala cried, "I'm going to...to...to..."

Cream gushed from her. She bucked, one hand slapping at the mat as her words became sounds. Just sounds. Sounds of pleasure that echoed through Torin's head, surged through his body, erupted in his groin. He curled his fingers into her hips, tore his mouth from between her thighs and—in one fluid move—rose up onto his knees and plunged his swollen cock

112

into her constricting sex.

"*Yes!*" she screamed, instinctively and instantly locking her legs around his hips. Her muscles closed around his thrusting length, tighter than tight, her wet heat scalding his craving flesh. He threw back his head and roared, unable to leash his pleasure anymore. The sound rent the air, rocked him to his core. He drove his cock into her pussy again, again, her cries and screams for him to fuck her harder, harder—"Oh, God, Torin, *harder*"—incinerating his control.

Molten steel flooded his balls. They rose up, pressed to his body, throbbed, ached. He slammed into her, wanting to be gentle, wanting to be savage. Wanting to take her to places of carnal rapture she'd never been, *he'd* never been before.

He pumped into her, filled her, possessed her. Claimed her. And just when he didn't think he could survive any longer, she thrashed her head side-to-side, arched her back and screamed once more. "*Yes yes yes yes!*"

Torin's release detonated. Rhythm deserted him. His seed pumped into Kala's centre, his arms wrapped around her waist, his sweat dripped onto her flesh. With one final roar, his body turned into a living fire of pure pleasure and he burned.

Ice-cold shadows reached for him, snaking over the floor, growing from the walls. He studied them, his muscles strung to breaking point, his blood roaring in his ears. Somewhere in those moving shadows, she waited.

He adjusted his grip on his sword and continued walking deeper into the chilling darkness, alert. Ready.

A trickle of sweat ran into his eye but he didn't blink or wipe it away. To do so would present a split moment of vulnerability. A split moment was all Kala needed.

The silence devoured the sound of his footfalls. Pressed down on him like a shroud. He raised his sword to guard, its hilt level with his chest, its heavy length parallel with his face. He saw nothing reflected in its silver length but the smooth stone walls and the suffocating shadows and his pulse quickened. He knew he was not alone, even if his eyes told him he was. He could feel her. She was here.

He lifted his sword a little higher, a little closer to his face, and he could almost believe the dead chill seeping into his cheeks radiated from its core. The sword had pierced more hearts than one weapon should, had spilled more blood than any other held by a *Sol* warrior and with every life taken it seemed to grow colder, as if infused with their displaced soul.

I've done this before, haven't I?

Torin moved further into the darkness and the shadows moved with him. Like tendrils of death he'd wrought on the worlds.

"You taint the air with the death that surrounds you..."

The words slid into his ear in an oily rasp, spoken...when? By whom? He narrowed his eyes. Where was he now? Where was—

A soft breeze caressed the back of his neck, played with his hair and he spun, sword tilted. Ready to deflect a strike.

Nothing filled the emptiness behind him. Just a long stretch of darkness never ending.

The shadows waited for him, their dense energy hungry.

Or was it what waited within those shadows that was hungry?

Hungry for him? Hungry for—

Is this is a dream?

The whisper of feet jerked him back around and he tightened his grip on his sword, straining to see her. She was there. He felt her. A molten heat in the crypt-like emptiness. A heat his own sought. Craved. Feared.

She was there.

Watching him. Waiting for him to—

A blinding wall of golden light flashed around him and he staggered backward, squinting into the glow, one hand raised to his eyes. His heart slammed against his breastbone and he dropped into a sprung crouch. He couldn't see. If he couldn't see, he was—

As quickly as it came, the light vanished, and he stood in the darkness again. Alone and unharmed.

He pulled a slow breath through his nose, his nerve endings like hot wire, and studied the shadows again. Where had the light come from? The walls themselves? What did it mean?

"It means the time is here."

He didn't recognize the voice breathing in his head, but he understood the words. He swallowed a thick lump in his throat and began to walk again. There was no other course. The seed had been watered. The perversion empowered.

I've done this before...

The shadows reached for him, growing hungrier. More insistent. His breath fell from his mouth in white mist, curling away from his lips in intricate patterns before dissipating to nothing. He frowned and lifted his sword higher, his gut clenching. There was meaning in those patterns, images he could not decipher. Images that would give him the answer, but he did not understand the question.

What question? Where was he?

I have. I've done this...

He quickened his pace, moving deeper into the icy bowels of the darkness, his grip on his sword growing painful. He had held it in his hands for a lifetime, an eternity. He could not remember a time when his fingers had not circled its hilt.

Yes, you do. When you found her. When you took her. When you pressed her to the floor and filled her with your seed. You did not hold the sword then. All you held was her. And you made her scream.

He stumbled over the whisper in his head and his gut clenched again. Syunna, what was—

Kala stepped out of the shadows, her hair a wild mane of black silk, her skin aglow, her green eyes incandescent. She looked at him and raised her right arm, the long sword she held horizontal in her hand smoldering with an inner heat that chilled him to the core. A sword made by the vengeful Eldest from the heart of existence to bring punishment on the worlds of man. "It is time, *Sol*."

Dreaming...

She swung the sword in a wide arc. Up behind her head and down over her shoulder.

Its long blinding-gold blade carved the blackness of the night in two, leaving behind concentrated fire and infinite energy.

Gods, am I dreaming again?

It sang as it did so, a thrum so deep and elemental, so powerful and potent, Torin felt the veins in his body quiver.

Again?

He dived away from its lethal trajectory, crashing to his shoulder and rolling across the cold granite floor, hot pain engulfing his neck and torso as he snapped to his feet and spun about.

She stood watching him, the sword waiting in her right hand. That she held it just with one hand alone made his mouth dry. She was small, so small, and the sword was so big. Too big. How was such a small slip of a thing able to wield such a weapon? It wasn't right. It wasn't fair. She was so small and the sword was so big.

I've done this...

She was so small and he was so big, so big. He towered over her and yet he'd held her, taken her, pressed her to the floor and filled her sex with his—

Her eyes flickered cold revulsion. "You gave your word." The sword ignited. Erupted in pulsing golden fury. "And you still made me scream."

She came at him again, hatred in her green eyes, the gold chips circling her pupils aglow with the contemptuous emotion, reflecting the blade's burning length.

...before. I've done this before.

The sword blurred in her confident grip, a deadly extension of her smooth, brown arm. He swung his own sword up into a counter attack. The edges struck and a violent shudder rocked existence. A pulse of silent sound, colourless light. He stumbled and Kala swung at him again, striking down in an arc of perfect rhythm and fluid grace. A searing jolt of pride stabbed into him—*he'd* taught her that—before he found his balance and deflected the blow. Just.

Once again, the world shuddered, as if two immense forces collided. Two elements never intended to meet.

A wave of scalding ice rolled over him, through him. His stare locked on Kala's, and for a frozen moment every molecule in his body seemed to shatter.

I'm dreaming. I'm dreaming.

He swung into a preemptive counter attack, slamming into her forward motion, his chest as tight as his grip on his sword's hilt. He cut the air with a sharp slice, his heart screaming at him, "No! You will kill her," even as his sword sped towards her head. She intersected the strike, the blunt parry jolting him off balance again. She came at him again and once more he was overcome with elated pride—his student, *his* student—as her blows forced him back a step. Another.

He raised his arm, drew guard, his knuckles popping, his shoulders burning as she rained down upon his sword strike after strike after strike.

The sword blazed brighter, hotter with each blow. He met each one, exhaustion tearing at his adrenaline, perverse joy feeding it. Her mastery was complete. She was everything the prophecy foretold. She was the weapon and the warrior.

As he had trained her to be so.

He had created her, forged her, taken her. Pressed her to the floor and made her scream.

"As the prophecy foretold."

The unknown voice drilled into his head and guilt claimed him. Cold and absolute. He faltered, his sword suddenly heavy.

Gods, I'm dreaming. Wake up.

Her sword sheared through the dark between them, wide to her side, down into a blurring arc and, before he realized what she was doing, its length drew under his arm and its blinding point sliced up his chest, cutting him open from nipple to shoulder.

He flailed backward, scalding agony searing through him, his stare locked on her face, her beautiful face, the face he would kill for. The face he would die for.

She threw herself forward into a cartwheel so quickly he didn't see her move before her heel smashed into the bridge of his nose.

I'm dreaming.

He went down. To his knees, blood oozing from the gaping wound in his chest, blood gushing from the shattered protrusion on his face.

Wake up.

His own sword, the one he'd used since he was twelve, dropped from his hand, sliding across the floor. Out of his reach. Lost in the shadows. Useless.

"I thank you, Torin Kerridon, last command warrior of the *Sol* Order." Kala Rei looked down at him, her eyes cold and merciless.

She leveled the point of the blade at the base of his throat. "For training me so well."

He lifted his chin high.

For the love of Syunna, wake up.

"You are welcome, False Fire," he replied.

Seconds before the woman he loved plunged the Sun Sword into his—

Wake up!

He jolted awake, gasping for breath. Sweat slicked his flesh, stung at his eyes. Syunna, the dream. The same gods-cursed dream.

A low whimper jerked his wide-eyed stare from the walls of the training room to the back of Kala's head. She lay on her side with her back to him, her hands tucked under her head, her knees slightly bent, her smooth brown skin somehow luminous in the room's muted light. An almost desperate need to feel her close gripped him and he slid his arm more firmly around her waist, drawing her body into the curve of his. Her bottom nudged his groin, her spine pressed his belly and she whimpered again, an almost inaudible hitching sound that made his chest ache and the pit of his belly stir.

"Shhh," he hushed quietly, stroking his fingertips over the smooth line of her ribcage. "Everything is well." The relaxed firmness of her muscles told him she was still asleep and he let out a ragged sigh, pressing his lips softly to the top of her head.

Fuck, the same dream. Why was he having the same dream?

He closed his eyes and immediately the image of Kala standing over him, Sun Sword blazing in her hands, cold hatred in her face, filled his head. She swung the sword in a graceful arc of absolute surety and terrifying beauty and plunged it into his chest—again.

Biting back a grunt, he opened his eyes and stared hard at the array of weapons mounted on the training room's far wall. Syunna, what was going on?

Pulse rapid, mouth dry, he smoothed his palm over Kala's belly, drawing comfort from the satiny warmth of her skin. She sighed in her sleep and wriggled closer to him, her bare backside rubbing his crotch with innocent friction. A wan smile pulled at his lips and he moved his hand up to the slight curve of her breast, brushing the knuckle of his thumb along its soft swell. She felt so good in his arms, so right. He'd never believed someone so small would fit so perfectly to his size and yet Kala did, as if they had been carved from the one piece of the old gods' stone. So why in all the hells was he having the same dream? Why would his subconscious keep telling him Kala was the False Fire? Keep torturing him with such a chilling notion?

"You gave your word."

An echo from his dream drifted through his head and a

heavy lump formed in his throat. He swallowed it down. He *had* broken his word, for the first time in his life, but he believed with every fibre in his body that he had not done the wrong thing. Kala had wanted him as much as he wanted her and he would not believe otherwise. The heady musk of her pleasure still lingering in the air told him as such. The way she'd moved beneath him, the way she'd held him, kissed him, told him his desire was not one-sided. No, his subconscious was wrong. He felt no guilt, only an overwhelming sense of rapture and peace. He *knew* who the False Fire was and the woman lying in his arms, her sweet scent tickling his nose, her gentle heat warming his body, her creamy pleasure wetting his thighs, was not the Eldest's perversion.

The False Fire was twisted by hate and fury. The False Fire was a creature of cruel lust and savage vengeance. The False Fire was bitter with contempt for mankind and hungry for its brutal demise. Kala was none of those things. The woman sleeping peacefully in his arms was kind and brave and stubborn and wonderful and...

"The One Who Burns," he murmured, lips pressed to the top of her head again. He drew a deep breath, letting the clean soapy scent of her hair filter into his body. He'd watched the inky-black strands grow over the last six months. Transform from a tangled, choppy mess barely long enough to hide her scalp, to a luxurious curtain of silk that tumbled around her shoulders when loose. He'd longed to bury his hands in its thick, glossy weight time and again, to feel its cool texture slide through his fingers, feather his bare flesh. He'd fantasized about it night after night, and now here he was, living those fantasies and yet the moment he closed his eyes all he could see, all he could live, was a lie beyond any nightmare.

The woman in his arms was not the False Fire. She couldn't be.

And still his chest ached from the memory of the Sun Sword puncturing his flesh, severing his muscle, his sinew, piercing his heart. And still his heart ached for the possibility he refused to accept.

"And still you made me scream."

Kala's tortured words from his dream scraped at his mind and he squeezed his eyes shut, denying them. No. He would not believe it. His head may try and tell him it was so, but his heart...his heart knew it was not.

The woman he had trained, the woman he desired above all else was *not* the False Fire.

Smoothing his hand back down to Kala's stomach, Torin gently tugged her closer, cradling her against the curve of his body. Her arse rubbed over his groin and she released another soft sigh, the contented sound curling his mouth into a small smile.

Torin released his own sigh. Despite the latent desire stirring in his sex at the intimate caress of her bottom, he let languid sleep steal through him, resting his lips against her head, his hands on her hip and waist. She was not the False Fire.

And nothing, not even his own guilt-ridden subconscious could convince him otherwise.

Kala opened her eyes, letting sleep's warm embrace slide away from her with contented calm. She smiled, stretching out her arms and legs, the flow of blood spreading through her exhausted limbs like a tingling caress. She rolled onto her side and tucked her hands under her head, grinning at the keeper of the Sun Sword's truth asleep on his side beside her.

"Well," she murmured, letting her gaze move over Torin's relaxed face, the glow of her numerous climaxes still warming her body. "I finally brought you to your knees in this training room of torture."

"See?" he murmured back, eyes still closed, the corners of his mouth twitching into a little grin. "I told you that you were a mighty warrior."

Kala laughed, the sound bubbling up her throat as wonderful as the pleasure Torin had given her. "I have a very, very good trainer."

Torin's grin spread into a wide smile and he rolled onto his back, threading his fingers behind his head and nodding with arrogant mirth. "Yes, you do."

Warm bliss rolling through her like the heat of a rising sun, Kala stretched out her right arm and rested her head on her biceps. She'd never seen Torin so relaxed. So completely at ease. The sight of his obvious contentment made her smile and a soft pulse fluttered deep within her sex. She pressed her thighs together, her nipples growing hard. She wanted to make love to him again. Now. She wanted to give Torin back the pleasure he'd given her.

You are going to kill him.

The Oracle's raspy voice whispered through her head and Kala's smile faded. The old woman had told her many things standing in the entryway of her cubicle, things that made little to no sense—a man who could not see was watching her; space would open and evil would step from within; she would be torn apart and remade; the heart of the future would ignite in the soul of the sword; the burning heart would pierce the undead heart and the *Sol* would live in the fire's flames—but Kala refused to believe any of it. They were the deranged ranting of an old hag who wore a dead rabbit about her neck. A dead rabbit! Ignoring everything else, what kind of savior was Kala meant to be if she was to kill the only person ever to show her kindness? The only person to show her true happiness? It was insanity to believe she would kill the man she loved. Lunacy to believe the very thing Torin had dedicated his life to would cause his demise.

Willing her uneasy tension away, Kala lifted her hand and traced her fingertips over the smooth curve of Torin's chest, along the white scars crisscrossing his flesh. Were they from battle? His own training? In time, could she ease the pain she saw in his eyes, take it away? Like he had taken away hers?

Did they have the time? Or was the damn Sun Sword and the fate of the worlds of man going to take that from them?

Don't let it.

She brushed her fingers over Torin's nipple, enjoying the way it puckered tight at her touch. The pulse between her thighs throbbed again—a little stronger, a little more insistent. Wherever they were headed, the seconds it took would be spent in each other's arms. "Make love to me again."

Torin turned his head toward her and opened his eyes. "Okay."

He rolled onto his side and slid his hand over her hip. Pressing his palm to the small of her back, he tugged her against his body, his lips feathering over hers in a kiss so reverent and gentle her pussy constricted with damp heat.

"I have believed in one thing and one thing only my entire life," he whispered, smoothing his hand along her spine, over the curve of her shoulder. "The Sun Sword." He skimmed the side of her breast with his fingertips before returning his hand to the small of her back, tugging her hips closer to the growing length of his erection. "As of this moment, I believe in nothing but you."

Kala traced her fingers over the hard muscles of his shoulder and met his unwavering gaze. "The One Who Burns."

Torin shook his head. "No, Kala. *You.*"

The flutter in her pussy grew stronger. "I love you, Torin."

His nostrils flared at her simple statement. He raised his hand and brushed her cheek with the back of his fingers, his gaze holding hers with unwavering heat. "You shouldn't."

She smiled, his raw claim making her throat tight. She could see the conflict tormenting him. She knew it all too well. Even now, with the warm glow of their pleasure still wrapped around her, still throbbing between her thighs, she couldn't believe what she'd longed for for so long had finally happened. Torin had held himself from her for six months, had believed himself her trainer, not her lover. She'd believed herself to be everything he didn't want. And yet here they were—together in such intimacy she never wanted the moment to end.

She lifted her hand to his and pressed it to her lips. "Yes," she murmured. "I should."

He closed his eyes, drawing a deep breath through his nose. "I have ached for you for what feels like a lifetime, Kala. Until you touched my soul I did not think it existed." He opened his eyes and looked at her, and Kala's heart leapt at the sheer emotion she saw blazing in their clear grey depths. "Until you found my heart I believed it to be stone." He cupped her face and brushed her lips with the pad of his thumb. "Until you knocked me on my arse I believed myself invulnerable."

"You still are," she said simply.

He smiled and shook his head. "No, not anymore. Not since I met you." He traced her bottom lip with his thumb again. "You've weakened me."

Before she respond—and really, what did she say to such a raw confession—he kissed her, his hand cradling her face with

125

tender care.

His lips moved over hers, gently, almost hesitant. As if he was tasting them for the first time. His tongue traced their inner line, flicked at her teeth. She drew in a quick breath and met his tongue with hers, equally as slow and tender. She'd never been kissed like so. It made her tremble. Made her feel cherished in a way she could not comprehend. God, she loved this man.

She didn't think she'd ever truly know how deeply.

For twenty-one years she hadn't believed the concept of love existed. Why would she? When all she'd known was hate and grief and pain? She'd never had anyone to love. She had no memory of ever being loved. Now she realized love had just waited for her to find it. In the heart of the known universes' last true warrior.

Torin's mouth journeyed her lips, branding them with infinite care, before he explored her jaw, her throat. He coaxed her onto her back with delicious pressure from his lips and she surrendered completely to his will. She stretched beneath him, her hands skimming his shoulders, down his back, over the blazing sun tattooed there, to his hips and back up again. "Please," she begged, her throat too tight for the word to be anything more than a whisper.

He lifted his head and gazed at her, his face solemn. "What, Kala?" His eyes seemed incandescent in the training room's muted light. "Please, don't ask me to stop because I can not. There is not a force strong enough in all the worlds to stop me making love to you."

She gave him a level look, struggling to constrain the urgent ache in her core. "I *am* asking you to stop, Torin." Sliding her hand up his arm, she caressed the hard curve of his shoulder, charting its firm muscles, exploring its latent strength. Everything about him spoke of power and brute force and it made her feel weak and strong at once.

His strength was hers. He'd given it to her in his passion, his desire and she wanted to give it back to him. Tenfold.

He shook his head, a stubborn denial pinching the side of his eyes. And a fear she recognized all too well. The fear of losing something so precious it was barely believed possible. "Please," he growled and she smiled, his very echo of her own plea filling her with a happiness she could no more understand than explain.

"There is something I need to do, *Sol*," she murmured, moving her hand to his neck. The rapid beat of his pulse danced beneath her fingertips, quickening her own, before she pressed her fingers flat to the side of his face. "Something that needs to be done."

The stubble on his cheeks and jaw scratched at her palm, heightening the pleasure rolling through her. Why, she didn't know. Maybe it was because she'd seen its prickling shadow many times before but had never felt it. To look at, the growth made him appear more menacing than facial hair should, but to touch...

A soft shudder claimed her body and she groaned. To touch, it was a confirmation of everything her heart knew to be true. He *was* strong and forceful and deadly, but with her, he was capable of softness beyond belief.

But now, now she wanted him hard.

She shifted beneath him, pushing him from her body. His eyes flashed with that same brittle fear she understood, but he did not offer any resistance. A low chuckle bubbled up her throat. That he didn't fight her made her love him more. She knew how much he wanted to sink into her heat and fill her and yet he didn't. He didn't protest. He let her rule him. She smiled, holding his gaze with hers as she rolled him onto his back. He had spoken at great length about trust during their training, and now he was showing his ultimate trust of her.

She looked down into his face and brushed her lips over his. "There is something I *want* to do."

Before he could ask her what, she straddled his legs, her thighs hugging his calves. Her gaze moved to his shaft and another groan rumbled up her throat.

He *was* hard. Hard and long and thick. And ready.

As was she.

She bent at the waist and took his length in her mouth.

"Gods!" Torin gasped, his whole body tensing beneath her.

She slid her lips down his cock, marveling at the satin smoothness of his straining flesh. It felt perfect, unmarred by scars and violence, its rigid strength radiating heat and urgent need. She rolled her tongue around its girth and slid lower, wanting to taste him all.

Torin groaned, his hands finding the back of her head. They curled into fists in her hair, holding her still as his hips lifted, thrusting his cock deeper into her mouth. Deeper.

"Gods, Kala, that feels..." His statement dissolved into a moan, the moan dissolving into a raw cry as the back of her throat pushed against his shaft's head. His fists tightened in her hair and he quivered beneath her, his leg muscles corded steel, his stomach jerking with shallow breaths.

She slid her mouth back up his length, pausing at the tip, flicking her tongue over the tiny slit there. Salted sweetness slicked her taste buds and she whimpered. He tasted of pleasure and desire and she wanted more. Shifting slightly, she pushed her right knee and then her left between his legs, kneeling in the V they formed. The position spread his thighs wide and she raked her hands down his torso, over his hips until her fingers found his silky pubic hair. She combed her blunt nails through the soft curls, enjoying the way Torin hitched a gasp every time her fingers drew close to the base of his cock. As if she stole his very breath from him with just her touch.

A liquid warmth flowed through her at the heady thought and she sucked on the distended head of his cock with greater pressure. She loved the way it felt in her mouth, how it fit so perfectly against the back of her teeth. She rolled her tongue over its satiny shape, tasting the small bead of his desire oozing from the tiny slit in its tip, before plunging her mouth down to his balls again.

"Syunna!" He bucked, ramming his hips upward, his voice a choked cry.

She didn't let him recover, sucking hard, taking him deeper. She raked her fingers over his groin, circling the base of his cock with one hand as she cupped and squeezed his heavy sac with the other.

"Fuck!" he ground out, thrusting upward again.

His cock rammed the back of her throat and, instinctively, she pressed her tongue flat in her mouth, granting his width full passage. He groaned, and held her head tightly, that salty-sweetness trickling from his slit as his cock stiffened in tiny spasms. He was close. She could feel it not just in the jerky pulses of his sex in her mouth, not just in the rising hardness of his balls in her hand, but in the thrumming tension in his muscles. In the way he gripped her hair and moaned her name. He was close to release, close to flooding her mouth with his seed.

That same warmth flowed through her again—wet and charged with elemental life. There was a power in what she did now to Torin she never believed possible. Not a shift in the balance of power, not a power of domination, but a power of shared connection. Of intimate respect and trust. Supreme trust. She'd thought he trusted her before, she knew he did now. And that knowledge pushed her closer to her own release.

God, I would die for this man.

Her heart smashed into furious flight at the realization and her head began to spin.

Sliding her lips from his length, she looked down into his eyes. She wouldn't just die for Torin—she would kill for him as well. He was her life. Her future. Her reason. He'd destroyed her old life and given her new purpose. Not the purpose of the Sun Sword, not the purpose of the *Sol* prophecy, but *her* purpose. To be with him. To love him. To share his life.

To share herself.

She pulled a shaky breath and gave him a serious smile. "For everything you have let me become, Torin Kerridon, I love you. For everything I am since you saved me, I love you."

Before he could respond, she moved from between his legs, raised her body from his and with a single, slow motion, impaled herself on his erection.

Pure pleasure filled her as completely as Torin's shaft filled her sex.

"Oh, gods," he groaned, his blunt nails digging into her arse cheeks. "Kala..."

His voice faded away on a ragged breath. His Adam's apple jerked up and down his strong throat and he closed his eyes, his nostrils flaring. She knew him well enough to know he fought with his control. She'd seen him do so time and again in this very room, fight to control himself. She'd always thought he was fighting to control his rage, fighting to control the desire to beat her to a bloody pulp. Never had she believed the battle he endured was the very same as the one she fought. A battle they had both lost. And won.

She shifted slightly, rising just enough to slide her sodden sex up his shaft. She felt its bulbous head stroke her within, its girth stretching her to the limit. Pushing her to the limit as well. She rose higher, her knees trembling not from exertion but from base pleasure, the lips of her pussy stretching wider as the head of Torin's cock broached her entry.

A raw groan rumbled up his chest and his nostrils flared again. He gripped her arse harder, his fingers digging into her tense muscles. "Don't."

She chuckled, the sound much more cheeky than she'd intended. "Don't what?"

His eyes opened and he looked at her, their grey depths so fierce her breath caught. "Don't move."

His voice shook and he held her motionless, his cock pulsing in her sex.

She wanted to obey him—she'd spent six months doing everything he commanded of her—but this was one order she could not follow. She'd never needed to disobey an order like she did his to stay still.

Her pussy constricted, squeezing the domed tip of his shaft, and she slid down its length.

Torin's jaw bunched. His eyes scrunched closed, his head rolled backward, the veins in his neck roped. "Fuck," he ground out through gritted teeth. His fingers drove harder into her arse cheeks, ten points of excruciating pain that filled her with exquisite pleasure.

Kala rolled her hips forward, pressed her clit to the base of his cock and then slid back up his rigid length once more.

"Fuck," he groaned again, eyes still closed, neck muscles

corded.

She smiled, her own muscles straining, each one coiled with searing tension, screaming for explosive release. How she controlled herself, she didn't know. With every stroke of Torin's shaft in her sex, the mounting tension in her body grew hotter. With every pass of his thickness against her drenched folds, the heat spread. Radiating from the junction of her thighs, prickling the base of her spine, pinching the tips of her nipples. She rode him, losing herself to the liquid fire sluicing through her body. She wanted to make this last forever, but with every thrust of his sex in hers she grew closer to the edge.

And she didn't care.

Because the moment he came, the second she climaxed, their battle would begin again and every orgasm they would mete upon each other's body was just a battle lost and won.

She withdrew up his length, a little, a little more, the soles of her feet burning, her pulse deafening her, and slid down again.

"Fuck, Kala!"

Up and down, slow and then faster. Faster. She studied his face, watched his expression. Tiny beads of sweat popped out on his forehead, his throat, slicked his smooth bronzed skin in a low sheen. She lowered her upper body to his, brushed her nipples over his chest. The moisture of his perspiration kissed each one and they puckered tighter, the training room's air chilling their damp tips.

Torin groaned, sliding his hands from her hips up her back. "Syunna, Kala." He sucked in a long breath and thrust into her sliding sex. "I can't last much longer."

She brushed her breasts closer to his chest and pressed her lips to the side of his throat, at the point where it became his shoulder. His skin was salted with his sweat, flushed with his pleasure. "Today we learn about control, *Sol*," she murmured against his neck, taking his cock deeper into her pussy as she did so. She moved her lips down to his collarbone, across his chest, sinking farther down his cock.

He growled, pumping his hips upward. "And you are my trainer?"

His strangled tone made her stomach knot with squirming anticipation. "Yes." She touched her tongue to his right nipple and he hissed in a sharp breath. "I am." She drew her tongue over his nipple again, flicked it before closing her lips around its rock-hard form and sucking gently.

A groan quaked Torin's chest, low and drawn out. She smiled and sucked again before sliding her mouth to his left nipple, nipping it with her teeth.

He groaned, muttering words she didn't understand but that made her sex heavy and wet all the same. She straightened a fraction, stroking his chest with her nipples again, a feather-light caress of skin on skin. The contact sent shivers of delight down her spine and her sex constricted, squeezing his cock with an insistent pulse.

Torin bucked, his fingers scraping at her back, a raw sound bursting from his lips. "Then I submit to my master."

With a slight shift of weight, she slid farther up his cock, moving her upper body forward as she did so, gazing into his eyes. She shook her head, her heart thumping so hard she wondered how it stayed in her chest. "Submission is not something I ever want from you, Torin." She inched higher along his erection, the rim of his cockhead stroking the walls of her sex unbearably erotic. "Ever."

His eyes blazed at her hoarse statement. "Good."

A shuddering force claimed him and his hands gripped her shoulders, slamming her into his penetrations. Her own pleasure rushed her toward the peak and she let it take her. Christ, she couldn't stop it. It was consuming her, filling her. Possessing her...

Exquisite tension detonated in her core and she cried out, her sex squeezing Torin's driving cock. Milking him of his spurting pleasure.

Pulse after rocking pulse claimed her, each one more powerful than the last, each one in perfect harmony with Torin's thrusting strokes. She shuddered with each until, drenched in sweat and rapture, she collapsed against him, spent and gasping and totally sated.

She lay against him, resting her cheek on his chest, the hammer of his heartbeat a sound of such wild, uncontrolled beauty she smiled. "Lesson finished," she murmured, turning her head to press her lips to his flesh in a soft kiss.

Torin chuckled, his fingertips skimming up and down her back in a slow, lazy dance. "You are a cruel trainer, Kala Rei."

She lifted her head and let him see her grin. "I have learned from the master."

"False Fire," a smooth male voice purred behind her.

Without thought or hesitation, Kala leapt upright, fists balled, muscles coiled. Instinctually and instantly ready to fight the intruder.

But Torin was on his feet before her, his eyes wide, confused, the blood draining from his face in a stunned pallor. "Seer?"

Kala spun around, adrenaline thumping in her ears. Her stare locked onto the ancient man standing on the mat but a few feet away and her gut rolled, inexplicable fear surging though her veins, turning her adrenaline to cutting ice.

Oh, God. Death has found me. Death has finally found me.

The old man's white, pupiless eyes flicked over her with overt disinterest, the air about him shimmering—as if space itself somehow opened around him—before he turned his attention to Torin. "No, *Sol*," he smirked, his right hand stealing to the rotting rabbit carcass hanging from his belt. "But I have been told the family resemblance is striking."

Stunned fury flooded Torin's face and he snarled, the sound more savage than any Kala had heard him make. "*Uloch.*"

The old man's smirk twisted. "So, my brother mentioned me."

"Only to curse your name."

"And yet, of us both he was the one to so misinterpret the prophecy." His white eyes flashed iridescent silver and he swung his stare to Kala, his feigned indifference gone. "Take her."

Two arms of steel clamped around Kala's torso, fingers just as hard snaring her chin and right breast, jerking her back against a body even harder. "I finally have you," a hot breath whispered in her ear. "False Fire."

"*No!*" Torin's roar ripped the air. "*Let her go!*"

From the corner of her eye, Kala saw him move. Lunging forward.

A burst of blinding white light filled the room, followed by a dull thud and the ancient man chuckled. "The Old Seer should have done more than curse my name, *Sol.*" He stepped forward, black coat billowing behind him, the stench of decaying meat wafting on the air. His stare focused on the floor behind Kala and he smiled. "Then you would have been more prepared. Now tell me where the Sun Sword can be found."

Kala struggled against man holding her, fighting his crushing grip with wild desperation. Her heart hammered. She couldn't see Torin. What was going on? What was that light? The thud? "Let me go, you fucking bastard."

"Not a chance, cunt. I have too much fun planned with you."

"*Let me go!*"

Uloch turned his head in her direction, his smile curling into an appraising grin. "I see the female's appeal, *Sol*, but is she worth it?"

"Yes."

Her throat slammed shut at Torin's choked voice. Why couldn't she see him? Was he hurt?

The fingers gripping Kala's chin dug harder into her flesh. "You feel worth it," her unseen assailant murmured. She thrashed in his hold, shards of cold pain spearing up into her jaw and skull. God, where was Torin?

What was going on? "Torin?" she yelled, bucking against the man. "Torin?"

Uloch's white eyes flickered silver again and his smile vanished, replaced with a vicious scowl. "Zroya will snap her neck and fuck her corpse, *Sol*, if you do not reveal the location of the Sun Sword to me now."

"Don't, Torin!" Kala fought against the man's—Zroya's— cruel arms. "Don't."

"Don't, Torin," Zroya echoed against her cheek in a perverted whisper, grinding his stiff cock against her arse.

"Speak, *Sol*." The old man's eyes flashed silver again. "Or watch her die."

Zroya pulled her tighter to his body, rammed his cock harder to her arse. "After I've had my fill of you."

"Speak, last command warrior of the *Sol* Order," Uloch stepped closer, stare locked on the floor behind Kala's feet.
136

"Keeper of the Sun Sword's truth. Or she is—"

"The second inner moon of P'helios."

Torin's strangled growl sank Kala's stomach and she threw herself against Zroya's arms. "No, Torin!" she screamed, fighting in the man's inescapable hold. "No!"

"The *Sol* Temple," Torin continued, his growl more choked. "In the Oracle's altar. Now, let her go."

The ancient man's scowl vanished, replaced by a wide grin of triumph. "No."

And with that, his eyes ignited with silver fire, the space around him unfolded and Kala felt her body erupt in agony as a million pinpricks of blistering white light tore her apart.

Chapter Six

Kala screamed. The painful light stabbed at her, swirled over her limbs, *through* her limbs, and suddenly she stood in a dark, cramped space that smelt of rotting meat.

Torin!

The frantic thought slashed into her horrified mind, chilling her blood...the second before she felt Zroya's body reforming behind her.

She slammed her elbow into his side, the impact like striking a wall of dense liquid steel. The man let out a surprised shout, the hard bands of muscles materializing around her torso flailing wide. Kala struck out again, smashing her fist into his still-translucent face, her knee into his gut, his nose.

He reeled backward, solid once more, frenetic pinpricks of light flaring over his flesh as he tumbled.

Kala fixed her stare on him, fists clenched, a distant part of her mind stunned at his breathtaking beauty, and drove her foot into his chest.

The force sent a shudder up her leg, into her belly. She watched him fall backward, hate and disgust heating her blood...

And was suddenly frozen.

"The prophecy is not wrong," Uloch's raspy voice oozed into

Kala's ear and the ancient man stepped in front of her, white gaze ablaze. "The False Fire *is* as strong as the One Who Burns." He smiled, yellow teeth glistening in the room's dim light. "Perhaps even stronger." He paused. "But not as strong as me."

Kala glared at him, fighting against the invisible force holding her motionless. Was he doing this? How? Who was he? What had he done to Torin?

Oh, God, Torin.

The thought of the *Sol* warrior ripped into Kala's fraying nerves. She fought to free herself, cold sweat breaking out on her forehead, her chest. A chill rippled her flesh and she realized she was still naked. Her heart thumped into her throat and she shoved the humiliating realization aside. "Let me go and I'll show you how strong I am."

Uloch's sightless stare razed over her like hot sand and her stomach twisted in revulsion. "Tell me, girl. Which of the prophecy's players do you think you are—the seed or the perversion?" He cocked a thin, wiry eyebrow. "The savior or the destroyer?"

"I don't give a rat's arse which one I am," Kala snarled, straining to move. "Just let me go."

Uloch chuckled, stroking his fingers over one of the rotting rabbits at his waist. "Oh, such a revealing answer. I wonder what my deluded brother would make of it if he were alive. The old imbecile was always a fool for the deceptive nature of words." He turned his gaze from her face and in the corner of Kala's eye she saw movement. Zroya had regained his feet and now stood by her side. "She needs to be alive when we reach P'helios." The innuendo in Uloch's command knotted her stomach and she struggled with a wave of sickening panic.

"Control yourself until then."

"Yes, my Master."

"I *will* kill you," she ground out, glaring at the old man, refusing to let the panic take her. "Give me half a chance and I will end your life."

Uloch turned back to her, expression pitying and conceited at once. "That is not the future *I* see."

"Then the future you see is wrong."

Zroya smashed his fist against her cheek and splintering pain flooded the side of her head. "You will not speak such to the prophet."

Blood pooled in Kala's mouth, coating her tongue with its coppery tang. She spat, ignoring Zroya as if he didn't exist, her stare still fixed on Uloch. "Such brave, brave men to attack a defenseless woman incapable of moving. Your balls must be made of brass."

Triumphant mirth fell over the old man's leathery face and he chortled. "The False Fire will speak with scathing contempt, the words marking the deceiver with death." His eyes shimmered silver and the force on Kala's body grew stronger. Crushing. "And the death of the *Sol* will mark the deceiver with pain and the Seer's power will be absolute."

Agony ripped through Kala's body and she grit her teeth.

No! I will not scream. I will not scream.

Pain consumed her. Held her captive. Hot tears squeezed from her eyes. Her breath squeezed from her compressed lungs.

God, Torin, is this what he did to you? Oh, God, Torin, no, no!

"Master!"

Zroya's sharp shout cut across the agony and suddenly the pressure vanished. Kala gasped, her body burning with pain, her soul burning with grief.

141

Oh, God, Torin. No.

Uloch stepped closer, eyes white once more, the stench of dead meat thick and cloying. He studied her for a long moment, his tongue flicking at the air, his clouded gaze roaming her face, and then, so quickly she almost missed it, a slight frown pulled at his forehead.

She bared her teeth at him in an icy grin. "See your future, old man?"

He spun away from her, black cloak billowing a wall of stinking decay, and left the dark space. Without another word. Without a backward glance.

Like an oiled snake, Zroya moved to stand before her. He skimmed one hand over her belly, up to her breasts, her throat. "You broke four of my ribs, False Fire," he murmured, fingertips stroking the sides of her neck in a gentle chokehold. His gaze roamed over her, his tongue playing with his teeth as he slid his hand back down over her breasts to her belly once more. "Now it's time for me to return the pleasure."

He smiled. And sank his fingers between her legs.

Just as Kala realized she could move again.

Torin forced the sluggish blood in his veins to flow through his numb limbs. He counted to one hundred, a slow count more torturous than the pain still trying to claim him.

Get up.

He ground his teeth, willing his fingers to move. Just one small twitch, that's all he needed. One small twitch and Uloch's dark magic would be defeated.

Nothing.

He pulled in a steady breath and the musky scent of Kala's pleasure, the salty tang of her sweat, filled his nostrils. The frozen pain in his body turned to a sickening tension. By the gods, Uloch had her. He had to get her back.

For the love of Syunna, Kerridon, get up!

The agony of the prophet's force rolled through him, its incapacitating power rending him heavy. The oxygen in his lungs felt thin, his head light. An invisible vise clamped around him, as if the very air tried to crush him. He stared at the training room's far wall, at Kala's training sword mounted there, the soft mat beneath him pressing into the side of his face. The scent of their lovemaking lingered on its surface, tormenting him. Haunting in its surreal reality. Only a moment ago he'd been lost in her body, lost in her pleasure. Only a moment ago she'd told him what he'd never dreamed he'd hear, her eyes shining with joy, her smile soft with contentment—*I love you.*

He bit back a screamed curse. He had to move. He had to get up.

Then do it, Torin Kerridon, the Old Seer's voice whispered in his mind. *Do not let my brother's trickery fool you. Remember your training.*

Closing his eyes, he formed a picture in his head—his hands, still on the mat, fingers splayed, motionless. He concentrated on them, forced them to move. Crushing weight pressed down on him as he did so, but he ignored it. His hands. The only thing that existed were his hands. He saw them in his head. Saw his fingers move, slightly at first, then with growing strength. Saw them wrap around the thick hilt of his own sword, the weapon he'd wielded since he was a boy, the same sword he'd used to prepare Kala for her destiny. Saw his knuckles bleached white as he tightened his grip and withdrew the heavy blade from its sheath. Saw his arms flex, his muscles bulge as he lifted the sword past his shoulder and plunged it into Uloch's chest.

He focused on the point of impact. Concentrated on the punctured flesh and bone and sinew. Let the mental image of the maniacal prophet's blood flowing from his body heat his own chilled blood.

Again, he willed his fingers to move.

Nothing.

This is not your training, command warrior. The ghost of the Old Seer's voice grew reproachful. *This is not your strength. Your strength is not your hate, Torin…*

Frustrated anger rolled though him and he wanted to scream again. How was he to save Kala if he could not move? How was he to save the woman he loved…

An image of Kala filled Torin's head—her warm body moving under him, her eyes alive with love, her lips parting with pleasure.

"I love you, Torin…"

Her murmured proclamation caressed his anger, a wave of sheer joy and living heat soothing his fear. She loved him.

A muscle in his left shoulder moved. Twitched. Bunched. He pictured Kala's smile. Heard her throaty chuckle in his head. Heard her murmur those words again—*"I love you, Torin."* His biceps coiled. Then his triceps, his deltoids. He pressed his palms flat to the training mat, life flowing through his limbs. She loved him. Kala Rei loved him. That gave him purpose beyond measure. Beyond magic.

He pushed himself to his feet.

Slicing energy surged through him and, like a million blades cutting into his very sinews, Uloch's magic fought to possess him again, to render him immobile. Like a river of acid flooding his veins, it tried to destroy him, but Torin denied its power.

Kala loved him. There was no magic more powerful than that.

He shoved himself to his feet and ran from the training room, the prophet's imprisonment holding him no longer. He had to get to P'helios.

The Old Seer had rarely spoken of his brother, but when he had his words had not been kind. Uloch was as brutal as he was obsessed with the Sun Sword. His methods of foretelling involved blood and bloody sacrifices. He read the entrails of not just animals but humans, specifically young woman, and took great delight in torturing those he deemed worthy of his "commune with the old gods". He had been severed not just from the Order of Seers but his family as well, over a century ago. The Old Seer grieved the loss of his brother and cursed him at the same time.

Torin bore no doubt Uloch would torture and kill Kala if it delivered to him that which he hungered so much. The Old Seer had warned him of such.

The shunned sightless one will paint the walls with the grief of the One Who Burns.

His gut churning, Torin pushed himself faster. He had to get to Kala. He had to—

Stop it.

Torin cut the frantic thought dead. Thinking of Kala in Uloch's possession would not help him. If he let his mind obsess on what the prophet was doing to her, what the man with the insane eyes who'd held her was doing to her, he would be undone. He needed to keep his head clear. Focused.

He stormed into the cockpit, dropped into the pilot's chair and punched in the co-ordinates. That he had traveled to the other side of the known universes to find the One Who Burns, only to return to his home planet, the home of the long-butchered *Sol*, for the final battle would have intrigued the Old Seer greatly.

A dark grin pulled at Torin's lips. There was a perverse rightness in the fact.

Leaning forward, he activated his ship's com-link and connected with the spaceport's command centre.

A low-pitched tone came over the link, followed by a thin metallic voice. "Ai'taina flight command. What is your request?"

"*Helios Blade* preparing to depart," he stated. "Request release of docking hold."

There was a dull clunk as the spaceport's docking hold deactivated. "Docking hold released, *Helios Blade*."

"Thank you, Ati'aina. Request permission to jump to immediate hyper-flight."

"Permission denied, *Helios Blade*. You will follow correct flight protocol and maintain minimum propulsion levels until two hundred kilometers from spaceport perimeter."

"No," Torin growled, cranking up his propulsion engines to maximum and preparing his body for the pressure about to hit him. "I won't."

He slammed the engine drive to full and *Helios Blade* punched a hole through time and space. Taking him to P'helios. To the Sun Sword.

To Kala.

Kala curled herself into a loose ball, hugging the thin cotton shift she'd found in the dark room closer to her body.

The metal floor ground against her hip, the garment offering little protection against its icy surface. She squeezed her eyes closed, biting on her bottom lip. Zroya was stronger than her. Stronger and faster. Maybe even faster than Torin. She'd never seen someone move with such frightening speed. Each punch and kick he'd delivered was like being hit with lightning.

Speed is not the weapon, Kala Rei. Strength is not the weapon. Focus. Belief. Picture the impact, believe in the strike. Know the end result in your soul.

Torin's instructions from their very first training session whispered through her head. She closed her eyes tighter, swallowing the choking lump in her throat.

What end result did she know now?

You are going to be killed.

She'd thrown everything she had at Zroya, every technique Torin had taught her, every move her own brutal upbringing had given her. She'd fought him to within a heartbeat from death and he'd defeated her. Had violated every part of her body for his depraved, sadistic pleasure. Used every part of *his* body to illustrate his power, his dominance over her, and when she'd remained silent, when she'd refused to call him the One Who Burns and beg his mercy, he'd done it all over again. And still, she didn't make a sound.

Not even a whimper.

A lifetime of being abused had prepared her. What Zroya did, he did only to her flesh. Her mind, her psyche, was shut to him.

Just.

"I *will* make you scream, False Fire," he'd stated with calm certainty, tucking his spent, flaccid organ back into his breeches. "I will make you beg for mercy." He'd studied her bleeding body, his handsome face pensive. "The mercy of the

147

One Who Burns is swift and just."

Kala glared at him through the sweat-tangled strands of her hair. "Remember those words, Zroya."

He'd laughed, a low, smug chortle that made her stomach knot and left her in the dark room, the seed of his debauched pleasure trickling down her thigh.

A moment later, a sickening jolt slammed into her body as the ship jumped into hyper-flight and she'd bitten back a choked sob.

They had taken her somewhere. Somewhere away from Torin.

The Sun Sword. P'helios' inner moon. The temple of the Sol.

Pulling her knees closer to her chest, Kala chewed harder on her bottom lip, willing the dull ache in her chest away. What did she do now?

"In your hands, Kala Rei, the Sun Sword brings ultimate judgment." The memory of Torin's words slipped through her mind, strong and absolute, bringing with them a bittersweet tension in her soul. He'd been angry with her when he spoke them. Very angry. They'd been seated in his ship's galley, their meal cold, the silence crackling between them. Once again she'd dismissed the Sun Sword and the prophecy of the One Who Burns and his invincible patience had finally cracked. *"The One Who Burns restores life where there is death. Brings death where there is life. The One Who Burns wields the power of the sun and you must accept that truth or all will be lost."*

She'd glared at him. She remembered that moment very clearly. She'd wanted to throw her plate at him. Four months into her training and she still could not fathom how a man like him could place his faith and devotion in something as ambiguous and nonsensical as a prophecy. Nor could she fathom how he could possibly believe she was the "One" the so-called prophecy carried on about.

She still couldn't. He'd turned her into a lethal warrior, he'd showed her what it meant to be worshiped, he'd given her true and absolute pleasure, but she still couldn't understand how he could believe she was the One Who Burns.

Her confusion was irrelevant however. Uloch had hurt the man she loved, possibly killed him. Zroya had defiled her and planned to do so again. There was no confusion about what she was to do next.

A cold sense of calm unfurled in her gut. Torin had trained her for one purpose and one purpose only—to be the wielder of the most powerful weapon in the known universes. Six months of her life had led to this moment. This truth. Whether she was the One Who Burns or, as Zroya believed with such fervor, the False Fire, she knew what she had to do now.

Closing her eyes, she rolled onto her back and began a slow count to one hundred, flexing and coiling the muscles in her body as she did so.

Her captors would come for her and they would take her to the sword Torin Kerridon believed hers to wield. Of that, she had little doubt. Uloch had ordered her kept alive for a reason and she doubted it was just to fulfill his puppet's sexual appetites. They would take her to the Sun Sword and she would take it in her hands—whether they wanted her to or not.

Until then, she would wait. And prepare herself for the weapon's final truth.

A cold, bleak smile pulled at her lips at the thought. "The One Who Burns' mercy *will* be just," she murmured into the darkness. "But it will *not* be swift."

Are you sure that's who you are?

Kala's smile turned bleaker. She honestly didn't care anymore.

What may have been short minutes or countless hours later, a deep rumble vibrated through the icy floor up into her body. She opened her eyes, welcoming the pulling sensation in her belly. The ship was coming out of hyper-flight.

She counted to one hundred twice, focusing on each muscle in her body individually, before a sliver of white light cracked the darkness to her right.

Kala folded herself into a sitting position, hooking her elbows around her knees to watch Zroya stride into the room. He stopped but a stride away from her, his gaze roaming over her with insolent arrogance. "I see you found the clothing I left for you. His lips curled into a smug smirk. "It is the attire of an Idekian slave." His teeth flashed in the dim light, his smirk stretching wider. "Quite befitting don't you think, given your position?"

Ignoring his provoking observation, she gave him a wide smile, flicking a quick look at the charged de-atomizer in his right hand. "A gun, Zroya? Really?" She let her smile turn nasty. "Your...sword...not good enough?"

He laughed, the sound empty and unhinged. "Now, you know better than that, False Fire. My 'sword' has already punctured your body and left you broken and bleeding. Shall I demonstrate its power again?"

Kala shrugged, keeping her face neutral. Relaxed. "If you feel you must. I have to admit though, I got bored the last time."

Zroya's handsome face became a mask of stunned disbelief and she suppressed the urge to attack. As much as she wanted to strike out and shatter his nose, his cheeks, his jaw, her body still needed to recover from the beating he'd given her. If she attacked him now, he'd defeat her once more. She couldn't have that.

"Use your opponent's weakness." Torin's voice. In her head.

Again. *"Watch for it and choose your moment well."*

Kala ground her teeth, her heart clenching. God, she wished she knew if he was alive.

Focus on the moment, Kala. On Zroya.

Her own voice reprimanded her and she returned her attention to the man standing before her. "Is there something you wanted, Zroya?" She cocked an eyebrow, letting him see her disdain. "Or can I go back to sleep?"

His fist smashed into her jaw. Almost too fast for her to see it move. "I look forward to seeing you grovel at my feet, Kala Rei. The cunt who dared pretend to be the One Who Burns begging me for mercy." His full lips stretched into a smile. "I especially look forward to denying you those pleas."

With blurring speed, he snatched a fistful of her hair and yanked her to her feet, grinning into her face. "Now, it is time. We have arrived and there are preparations to be made." He jerked her closer, so close she could smell his putrid breath. "Ready for the fun to begin?"

Kala moved her face closer still, letting her stare drill into his. "Absolutely."

He spun her around and shoved her from the room, the de-atomizer's barrel digging into the small of her back.

Marching her through the ship, he said not a word. Kala felt his strung energy radiating through his body, down his arm, passing through the weapon he rammed against her back. That he carried a gun at all told her he was nervous. A small smile played with her lips. Good. She liked that.

"The False Fire is ready, my master," Zroya suddenly spoke behind her and Kala realized they'd stopped in the very room in which she'd first arrived on the ship.

The stench of decaying meat wrapped her in a choking

blanket.

"You have done well, child." Uloch's raspy voice scratched at her right and she turned her head, finding the withered old man standing beside her, stroking a freshly gutted rabbit. His gaze skimmed over her and if he noted the blood seeping from her nose, the bruises marring her cheek, he showed no signs. "The False Fire will serve us well. And when the Sun Sword is free, when it is in the hands of the One Who Burns, Zroya, you may do with her what you will."

The shift in the de-atomizer's pressure told Kala that Zroya had bowed. "I eagerly await that moment, my master."

The old man smiled, his white eyes holding her gaze, his tongue flicking at the air. "The severed brother shall reap the rewards denied him of his kin," he murmured, expression unchanging, "the departed brother's charge rendered impotent by the weakness of his want, the sleeping blade awaiting to be claimed."

Kala threw Zroya a look over her shoulder. "Is this the way he always speaks? Or am I getting special treatment?"

Uloch's smile vanished. "Enough." He lifted one hand. "The prophecy calls."

Without warning, Zroya smashed the butt of his de-atomizer against the back of Kala's head. She sank to the ground, black blotches of pain detonating in her vision, her knees and palms connecting with the icy metal with a crack.

"Fuck," she burst out, glaring up at the leering Zroya as he sauntered around to stand before her. "A little heads-up would have been nice."

His stunningly handsome face twisted with sadistic mirth. "Oh, sorry, cunt." He bent at the waist to gaze into her face with melodramatic sympathy. "I'm going to hit you now." He laughed. "Better?"

Kala smiled. "Much," she said and slammed her forehead into his nose.

"You fucking—" Zroya staggered backward, eyes wild, blood gushing down his face.

"Zroya." Uloch's rasp stopped him.

A vicious snarl split Zroya's face. He stared at Kala, hate and bloodlust burning in his glare. "I apologise, master."

Kala gave him a wide grin, ignoring the dull ache in her forehead and the sharp pain in the back of her head. "I don't."

"Your bravado is to be commended, Kala Rei." Uloch moved to stand before her, Zroya bowing out of his way. He studied her, stroking the gutted rabbit's hollowed out innards, his fingers playing over the creature's ribcage in rapid twitches. "But it is unnecessary. What is to transpire requires nothing of you except your presence."

"If it's all the same to you, I think I'll pass."

The old man chuckled. "The prophecy does not give us such choices, Kala Rei." He caressed the ribcage of the dead rabbit again, fingertips slicked with sticky blood.

Kala raised an eyebrow, watching the movement of his fingers with rising curiosity and growing unease. "So, is now a good time to tell you I don't believe in the prophecy?"

Uloch chuckled again. "Let me change that for you." He nodded, his eyes firmly fixed on her face. At the slight action, Zroya moved behind her and snaked his arms under her armpits, jerking her to her feet. She bucked, fresh pain stabbing into the back of her head, but Zroya only laughed and yanked her harder to his body.

"When this is done," he murmured in her ear, "I will tie you to my whipping post and show you what my...sword...is truly capable of."

Kala ground her teeth, staring hard at the old man standing before her. "Promises, promises."

Uloch dipped his hand deeper into the rabbit's guts, his lips moving with silent words. He took a step closer to her, his stare boring into hers. "With blood shall be seen pain," he rasped, withdrawing his hand from the dead animal's carcass. "With pain shall be seen past." Eyes clouding, he reached for her head with blood-stained fingers.

No. Kala bucked in Zroya's hold, fighting his cruel arms. She did *not* want Uloch touching her with those fingers. She did not—

His fingertips brushed her cheeks just below her eyes and red agony sheared through her. Paralyzing her. Consuming her and she was...

She was afraid. She cowered under the broken bed, eyes squeezed shut, biting her lips as the men threw her mummy across the room. Her mummy had told her not to make a noise—"You need to be quiet, honey, quiet like a little mouse. Don't make a noise, Kala-bear and it'll be fine"—and she was trying, she really was, but all she wanted to do was run to her mummy and make the men go away. Tears stung her eyes. Snot burned her nose. She cowered lower, her hands balled into fists, her heart thumping in her throat. She wished her mummy had never brought her here, but they had nowhere else to go. The sickness had come to their town and they'd had to get away before it got them too. Now the men had found them and she knew what they wanted to do.

A scream tore the air, her mummy's scream, followed by a laugh that made her tummy roll. "You want this, cunt. I know you do," one of the men said and she heard a wet, meaty whack. Her mummy screamed again, the sound cut short by another whack. "Hold her still, for fuck's sake," the man grunted. "She's gonna kick me balls off!"

She bit her lips harder, blood coating her tongue as she rammed her fists to her ears. She wanted to run away, but she couldn't leave her mummy. She couldn't go. Her mummy had told her to stay quiet. The tears squeezed from her eyes and, before she could stop it, a high whimper vibrated in her throat.

"Oi," one of the other men burst out. "There's someone else 'ere."

The second he uttered the words her mummy screamed: *"Kala! Run!"*

She squirmed from under the bed and leapt to her feet, running for the gaping doorway on the other side of the derelict shack. The biggest man leapt at her, rotting teeth flashing in the dying sunlight. He snared her long plait and yanked her backward.

"Leave her alone, you bastard!"

Her mummy's screech tore into her terror. Petrified, she thrashed in the big man's arms, kicking, squealing. He laughed and threw her at the man with the sores on his face. "Bit of dessert for us, mates," he chuckled.

The skinny man's hands ripped at her clothes and she grabbed one of his arms, sinking her teeth into his filthy skin.

"Fuck!" He flung her away. "The little cunt bit me!"

"Leave her alone!" her mummy cried, her voice high and broken. "Oh, God, please, leave her alone."

She scrambled up and threw herself at the laughing man, punching him as hard as she could. "Let my mummy go! Let my mummy go!"

He laughed again and hauled her off the ground by her hair, her long thick hair. "How bout we go with you first then?"

"*No!*" her mummy screamed. "You leave her alone, you bastard! You leave her alone!"

The big man tossed a look over his shoulder at something she couldn't see. "Shut her up, will ya, Macca."

A solid crack broke the air and suddenly she couldn't hear her mummy anymore.

"Mummy?" Terror welled up in her belly. Stole her breath. "Mummy?" She kicked out, slapped her fists against the man's arm. Tears burned her cheeks. "*Mummy?*"

"Got me a little piece of girlie-girl, mates." The big man grinned, throwing her to the ground. He slammed his foot into her tummy and blood burst from her mouth. "She's gonna be tight, real tight." He stood over her, his feet on either side of her hips, grinning down at her. "And I get first go."

Hands grabbed at her. Horrible hands with ragged, dirty nails. Horrible hands that grabbed her wrists and rammed them into the filthy floor. Horrible hands that grabbed her ankles and jerked her legs wide apart. "Mummy?" she squealed. "*Mummy?*"

The big man laughed. "Call me daddy, girlie-girl."

And he dropped down on top of her and she...

She gasped, jolting in Zroya's hold. She glared at the old man before her, her heart a pounding sledgehammer trying to smash free of her chest. "What the fuck did you do to me?"

Uloch gave her a small smile. "Well, that was interesting, wasn't it, child?"

Hot rage poured through her, turned her blood to acid. She threw herself at him but Zroya's arms locked tighter under her armpits. "You bastard!" Her roar tore her throat. She thrashed in Zroya's grip, teeth bared, stare locked on the smiling prophet. The freshly exposed memory devoured her. Tore her apart. Memories she'd long ago buried deep within her tormented soul. Everything about that day came back to her in a tsunami of senses. She couldn't escape. Not then, not now. "You fucking bastard."

Uloch tilted his head to the side, fingering the rabbit carcass. "Such a young thing to experience something so brutal." He lifted his hand and Kala flinched. "So heinous."

Zroya chuckled behind her, the low sound vibrating through her body. With each tremble, she felt his erection nudge her arse, and a wave of contempt and hate rolled over her. She ground her teeth, refusing to break Uloch's stare. "What doesn't kill us only makes us stronger."

He raised his eyebrows. "A commendable attitude toward something so barbaric. Do you think your mother shared the same sentiment? Or was the last thing on her mind as the men fucked her to death the screams and sobs of her daughter?"

Kala glared at him, straining against Zroya's hold. She could hear the woman her traumatized psyche had erased from her mind crying in her head. Begging, pleading. Bargaining for Kala's life even as the men violated her until she was silent. Each sob sliced into her. Cut her. "Shut up."

"Did they even let you see her body before they took you away?" he went on, a quizzical, almost concerned expression on his face. He stroked the rabbit's matted fur. "Did they let you say goodbye to her lifeless corpse?"

She clenched her jaw, her nostrils flaring. "Shut up."

"How long did they keep you for, Kala? How long did those men use you for their own gratification?"

"Shut up."

"Was it days? Months?" He brushed one long red-slicked fingertip down the side of her face. "Years?"

Kala narrowed her eyes, a prickling fire razing over her flesh. Memories assaulted her, but she shut them from her mind. Her soul however... "Days," she snarled.

"How many?"

"None of your business."

Uloch traced another line down her face. "I can find out if you like, Kala Rei. We can revisit each one. Linger on every minute if you so desire."

Terrified fear and incinerating fury destroyed her. She turned wild, bucking, kicking, throwing Zroya off balance. *No, no. Not again. Not again.* He hauled her feet off the floor, laughing and then slammed them back down. The shock jarred her ankles, her knees. Her hips screamed. Her spine buckled. She cried out, tears squeezing from her eyes.

"Hush," Uloch crooned, fingering the rabbit carcass again. "We have more to do. More to see." He raised his blood stained hand to her face, his eyes growing cloudy. "With blood shall be seen pain. With pain shall be seen fate."

She shook her head, Zroya's erection drilling into her as she shrank from Uloch's fingers. *No. God, no. No.*

He touched her chin, shoved his fingers to her lips, into her mouth. Putrid rot oozed over her tongue, slipped down the back of her throat and she...

She ran, the man chasing her. He shouted at her, called her vile names, yelled vile words at her back—what he was going to do to her when he caught her, what he was going to make her do to him. She ran, her heart thumping in her throat, making it hard to breathe. She thought she'd been safe hiding in the collapsed building's basement. She thought she could sleep, rest. She'd been wrong. A stitch speared her side, ripping deeper with every gasp she pulled. This is what she got for

158

becoming complacent. This is what she got for thinking she was finally safe. Months and months of being left alone and thanks to one moment of sheer complacent stupidity the man had seen her. God, she had to get away. She couldn't let him catch her. She couldn't...

She couldn't fight them. There were too many. "Gotcha, cunt," the man with the knife sneered. She pressed her back to the crumbling brick wall behind her, her stare darting from one salivating, leering man to the other. Five of them. Five. Her ankle screamed at her and she knew it was broken. How was she to fight them with a broken ankle?

You just do, Kala. You never give up. Ever. After all these years you know what to do. Shut out the pain. Kill it. Or let it kill you.

"Gonna have some fun now, cunt." The man stroked the edge of the knife with his thumb, his face splitting into an obscene grin. His companions guffawed, two of them taking a step closer to her. They eyed the steel pipe in her hand. She'd blinded one of their number three days ago when they'd first stumbled upon her and their hesitation was evident. But she was outnumbered. And trapped. And injured.

"Gonna fill you up to the eyeballs, cunt," the man went on. He didn't move. He didn't have to. He knew she was caught as well as she did. He knew she was...

She was screaming. The old woman was screaming.

"Please, please!" the old man cried, his kind, sweet eyes red with tears. "Please, don't hurt her." The man with the metal arm hit him, smashed him in the side of the head and he fell, blood bursting from his nose. Kala stared at the old man lying motionless on the ground, at the blood pooling beneath his head, at the tears slipping from his blank eyes.

"Why do you cunts always scream?" the man with the metal arm said. He stepped over the old man and grabbed a fistful of her hair, forcing her to look up at him. "As if it ever..."

She was chained to the wall. She yanked on the rusty length, her torn, bloody hands slipping over the steel. Five nights, five days, chained and starved and used. Five nights, five days. Who knew how many more to come? A sob threatened to escape her but she bit it back. Fucked if she was going to cry. Fuck them, if they thought chaining her up in an old abattoir would make her cry. Or scream. Or make it easy for them. If they wanted to stick their dicks between her legs again they'd have to...

Laughter. His smug laugh cut into her agony and turned it to something darker. Hotter. The bastard leered down at her, shoving his flaccid cock into his trousers before kicking her in the ribs. She ground her teeth, her scream trapped in her throat. "Try an' enjoy it next time, will ya?" He spat, the wad of phlegm landing on her cheek. "Ya takin' the fun outta it all."

She glared up at him. Her blood ran down her face, into her eyes, coating them in a stinging red film. "Maybe if you had a dick I would," she snarled. "Instead of that limp growth dangling between your legs. Seriously, I've seen dogs better hung than you."

Indignant disbelief twisted his face and he swung his foot into her side again.

She grabbed his ankle before the toe of his boot could slam into her ribs, the chains around her wrist shearing into her flesh. She didn't care. She didn't feel the pain. Only the burning fury. Fury was all she had now. All she needed.

160

He stumbled back a step, throwing his arms in wild arcs in an effort not to fall, jerking his ankle free of her grip. "Why you fucken'..." He didn't finish, at least not with words. His foot smashed into her stomach, her chest. He stomped on her hands, her fingers. She heard them break but didn't feel the pain. Only the burn of her rage. Only the...

"The fire."

Uloch's whisper stabbed into her ear. She jerked backward, Zroya's arms clamping tighter around her chest. Sweat trickled down her face, into her eyes, over her cracked lips. She stared at the old prophet, agonized torment consuming her. A lifetime of the vilest abuse, the most horrific existence. From the first to the last. He'd made her live them again. Her nightmares. Her memories. Her truth. A lifetime of memories she'd denied every minute of every day. Memories she would give anything to destroy. Memories she believed Torin had extinguished with his kisses, his touch. Fury razed through her. Turned her blood to molten hate. "You bastard," she gasped.

"The *Sol* prophecy sees me differently, Kala Rei." He brushed a tangled strand of her hair from her forehead with the back of one bloody knuckle. "It sees me as the deliverer of the Sun Sword's true wielder."

Zroya chuckled behind her, grinding his dick into the base of her spine. "That would be me, bitch," he murmured in her ear.

Uloch smiled, his stare boring into Kala's eyes. "It has taken a lifetime, Kala Rei, to make you what you are. From your birth to this very moment."

She sucked in a slow breath, her scalding hate wrought by the torturous memories churning through her. "And what's that, old man?"

His smile stretched wider. "Mine."

She snarled. "Fuck you."

He slid his white stare to Zroya and back to Kala again. "It is time." He skimmed the back of his knuckle over her cheek, an obscenely tender gesture that made her gut twist. "For the One Who Burns and the False Fire to stand before the Sword."

His face went slack, his eyes clouded, there was a dull *pop* and Kala's body suddenly erupted in a million pinpricks of agony and light.

Chapter Seven

She gasped, every molecule tearing apart as the space around her folded.

Nothingness suffocated her. Black pressure blinded her. She screamed, the silent sound torn from her throat, piercing into her ears. Her atoms disintegrated and she became the space, the nothing.

And then she opened her eyes and gazed at the cavernous hollow in which she stood.

Smooth rock walls rose high above her in a gentle curve, so high shadowy blackness hid their apex. Their surface glowed a muted golden light that seemed to emanate from the stone itself and illuminate little.

Where...? Kala pulled a quick breath, icy air streaming down her throat into her lungs.

A ripple ran over her flesh, pinching her nipples tight and, despite the chill, a simmering heat unfurled deep in the pit of her core, licking at every nerve ending in her body like singeing embers of a growing force tasting her from the inside out.

She frowned, a soft beat fluttering in her neck. What was going on?

The beat quickened, filling her throat, thumping in her ears. She gazed at the glowing walls, their stretching span hurting her eyes. It was like looking at a lie. No space could be so immense and yet so oppressive. Another ripple coursed over her, making her nipples ache and her hair stand on end. The freezing air turned colder, even as the embers in her body grew hotter. Turned to fingers of heat that seeped into her existence. Seeking, seeking...what?

What is *this?*

"The Sun Sword calls its destiny." Uloch's elated proclamation came through the heat building within her. She flinched, the sound of his voice faint and yet somehow amplified in the cavernous corridor. *All* sound cut into her ears, each noise, no matter how soft, sharper in clarity than ever before. She could hear Zroya's shallow, rapid breaths slip past his nasal hairs, over the skin of his nostrils. She could hear Uloch's heart beating inside his chest. She could hear his blood surging through his veins, being sucked into his black heart and spat out again.

Heightened beyond possibility, every one of her senses assailed her. She could smell Zroya's clammy sweat beading on his forehead. She could smell the old dried blood rusting on Uloch's cloak. She could taste the ice on the stagnant air, the metallic mix of blood and snot in Zroya's clotting nose. With each step she took, she could feel the vibrations of the two men's footfalls tickling the soles of her feet. With each step deeper into the darkness, she could see the shadows around her writhe and shrink from the glowing walls.

No, you can't. You're going insane. It's all been too much, too much and your brain has finally—

Heat rolled through her, a wave of unadulterated warmth that stole her breath.

God, she was burning. Burning from within. Something had set her alight. Something unseen. Something...

She stood still, the flames devouring her soul. Devouring her.

Is it...?

The junction of her thighs grew heavy. Wet. Hot.

Is it...?

She sucked in an icy breath, her lungs on fire. White-hot pressure curled around her heart, into her core, and her lips parted.

Oh, Torin. I can feel *it.* Her sex throbbed. Her palms itched. Her blood roared in her ears. *It's here. I can feel—*

"We move."

At Uloch's utterance, barely audible through the heat devouring her, Zroya shoved Kala forward. She stumbled from her frozen stance and a scalding fist buried in her belly. Holding tight.

Pulling her. Taking her.

They walked through the cavern, their footfalls like the sound of cracking ice, the fist in her belly squeezing tighter. More insistent. Demanding.

Demanding what? What is it? What is going on?

No answer came to her. Instead, a prickling weight pressed at the back of her head and she lifted her face to the walls around her.

Row after row of men stared down at her. Massive warriors carved into the rock, watching the perverse procession beneath them with calm faces and empty eyes. She gazed at them, noting their menacing physiques, the swords of different lengths and widths that they each gripped, the various images of blazing suns on various parts of their bodies. Kala felt their lifeless stares raze her flesh and, without understanding how, she knew immediately these men were the fallen *Sol*. The warriors of whom Torin had spoken, killed by a single command from the Oracle.

A tingle traced up her spine and her already aching nipples puckered painfully. They studied her, the carved *Sol*. Assessed her. She didn't know how, but they did. They weighed her and measured her as she walked beneath their forms. She frowned, studying them in return, and a deep sense of grief blossomed in her chest, rivaling the fist in her gut. *Oh, God, Torin...*

His name filled her head, flowed through her body like the caress of cool water over parched lips.

Her throat grew thick and she turned her stare from the warriors. Their grief called her, recognized her and she bore it. She knew what they wanted her to do. The furious ache in her soul for the man she loved told her so. The hideous memories Uloch had awoken in her told her as well. She needed to keep her focus. The scalding fist in her belly tugged with greater urgency, the pulse in her sex throbbed with stronger need— *Come. Hurry.*

"The blade shall mark the One," Uloch whispered behind her, the excited words tripping over each other. "And the One shall mark the blade, and the fire shall burn and the sightless one shall become one with the power and the worlds shall feel his ascension and..."

A soft tone threaded over the old man's feverish voice, low and almost inaudible but there all the same. It brushed Kala's mind like particles of mist. She shook her head. Frowned.

"...and the one who stood alone will bleed and the blood with give birth to the fire and the truth and the death will give birth to the..."

The tone grew louder. Kala scrunched her face. It was in her ear. In her head. It was—

"...the blade will sing and the song will call and the One

Who Burns will see..."

The tone rang louder. Louder. Like a million voices all singing as one. A choir of voices singing one word. Drowning Uloch's words in a pure, golden note.

Oh, Torin. What is going on?

The thought barely penetrated the rising tone. She swayed on her feet, the sound of Torin's name in her head making her stomach clench.

Torin.

His name echoed in her mind again. Rising over Uloch's ranting drone. Threading through the pure tone. Through the singing. A complementing accompaniment that made her sex throb harder.

Torin.

"...blood on stone, blood in stone, the One Who Burns will know true fury..."

Torin.

"...will unleash and the one who stood alone will..."

The singing rose higher. Louder. Louder. A deafening choir of infinite harmony. Kala lifted her hands, desperate to press them to her ears, to block out the sound, the pure, terrifying sound, but Zroya rammed his gun harder into her back. His fingers dug into her biceps and he jerked her backward a little, enough to make her footfalls stumble. "Uh-uh."

His smug reproach barely penetrated her head. The singing filled it, filled her, and now she could distinguish the words of the mellifluous song.

Here here here here here

One word, a million voices, singing a single word. Yet through it all, overlaying each note, each crescendo and each diminuendo Kala could hear a lone voice speaking one name.

One name, spoken with such ethereal strength Kala could barely draw breath—*Torin.*

She lifted her head, raising her gaze to the carved *Sol* watching her grim march through the temple. Their grief still pressed upon her, an infinity of loss and despair for their last warrior. She followed their frozen presence, studied each one as she walked beneath them. Marked each one. Just as they marked her.

Here here here here here.

The song grew louder, more rapturous. Exultant. Kala's feet moved of their own accord, the burning fist in her belly no longer pulling her, but guiding her. No longer drawing her through the temple, but welcoming her.

Torin.

Torin.

She studied the carved *Sol* staring down at her, letting their grief seep into her core, taking it as her own. Until she came to the last one and her heart leapt into her throat.

Torin.

He stood at the end of the silent procession, his image chiseled into the glowing stone, his powerful energy undeniable even in such lifeless medium. In his right hand rested a blazing sun, the golden light of the walls seeming to radiate from its spherical shape. In his left hand rested a bleeding heart, drops of carved blood trickling down his wrist and forearm as if to fall from his elbow onto the massive black stone altar shrouded in shadows beneath.

The Oracle's altar.

"The Sun Sword," Uloch cried, and a chill shot through Kala.

She blinked, and just like that the inferno in her body was

extinguished, the singing in her head was silenced. Gone. She frowned, the pit of her belly knotting. Had they ever been there?

Yes, they had, Kala. They had. If not, you truly have gone insane.

The thought chilled her further and she frowned again, staring up at the image of Torin before her. He looked down at her, his eyes piercing and commanding, and her heart cracked with utter despair. "Torin," she whispered.

Unable to look at him any longer, she dropped her gaze to the dark altar before her. The shadows seemed to move there, charged with life beyond her sight and understanding, and an empty longing curled around her heart.

She was alone. Wishing for life where she knew there was none, aching for an ending that could never be. Even the euphoric singing had become ominous silence.

She pulled an icy breath and let her grief feed her rage. Uloch had brought her to the weapon she had been trained to wield. Soon she would use it to end it all.

"The One Who Burn's mercy shall be just," she murmured on a breath, a dull heat beginning to unfurl deep within her once more. "And bloody."

A shift behind her jerked her stare from the shadow-shrouded altar and she watched the prophet step past her, his gaze fixed on the stone formation. "And the spurned brother shall find the Sword," he intoned, his arms wide, a dead rabbit in his left hand, "and the One Who Burns shall wake it from its cold slumber and all hearts shall beat again."

"Well, all hearts except yours, Uloch," a deep voice said, and Kala gasped as Torin stepped from the shadows of the altar into the light. His eyes burned grey fire and his lips curled into a cold smile. "And the walking corpse who dares touch Kala Rei."

His left arm moved so quickly it was just a blur. Something small and silver shot from his hand, slicing the air with a hiss. There was a wet thud, a sharp crack and, as if it had suddenly sprouted from his body, Torin's gutting knife hilt jutted from Uloch's chest.

"No!" Zroya screamed.

Kala spun, smashing her fist into his face. The man's head snapped backward, blood spurting from his nose. Glistening beads fanned above his head in a grotesque crimson arc before, eyes murderous, handsome face distorted with fury, he locked his stare on hers and slammed the barrel of his de-atomizer to her forehead. "Die, cunt."

"Cease."

The single word cut the chaos like a detonation, and Kala couldn't move.

Uloch stepped up beside her, those hideous white eyes of his shimmering iridescent silver light. He lifted his hand and traced his fingertips down the side of her face with gentle care. "She is needed." He swung his head slowly toward Torin, who stood frozen—mid-lunge, sword drawn—before the *Sol* altar. "You," he continued, lips pulling into a cold, smug smile, "are not."

The pressure trapping Kala vanished and everything moved again. Everything. Including the blade buried in Uloch's chest.

It burst free of its fleshy sheath, sucking blood and ichor with it. It moved so fast Kala could not track its projection. The blade shot through the air, sinking hilt deep into Torin's throat.

She screamed.

Torin's eyes grew wide. Blood bubbled past his lips, bright red and frothy. His stare swung to her, his bloody lips parted and, knife buried in his neck, he fell backward onto the stone altar.

170

"No!"

Kala leapt for him, every fibre of her being denying what she saw. Refusing to process it. No. It couldn't be true. No.

Behind her, Uloch laughed, the sound high and wild. "A physical weapon will not kill me, *Sol*," he crowed. "I am the prophet. I transcend the physical, the laws of reality, a gift from the old gods my short-sighted, thoughtless brother should have mentioned while cursing my name." He laughed again, a gleeful screech of smug triumph. "And as the prophecy has foretold, the lone warrior's blood will be spilled and the last of the *Sol* will be no more!"

No no no!

Blood trickled from Torin's mouth and down his chin. Kala ran for him, her heart hammering. No. He wasn't dead. He wasn't. He wouldn't do that to her. He wouldn't leave her like—

Someone grabbed a hank of her hair and yanked her off her feet. "I'm going to fuck you on the *Sol*'s bleeding corpse, False Fire," Zroya snarled, slamming his foot into her stomach as she hit the ground. "And then I'm going to break your nose and fuck your face just for some fun."

He slammed his foot into her side again and Kala bent into the blow, grabbing his calf, glaring up into his shocked face. She grinned, the action awakening something dark and scalding within her soul. "Going to be hard to do that after I rip your pathetic dick from your body, Zroya."

She threw his leg away from her, using his weight as a counter-pivot to spin herself to her belly. She was on her feet before Zroya could recover his balance. Hot hate consumed her. Filled her. She stared at him, the fire in her blood alive. The agony in her heart was absolute. Absolute.

Oh, God, Torin.

"And the False Fire shall be destroyed by the One Who

Burns and the One Who Burns shall perish to the False Fire."
Uloch's whisper slithered into Kala's ear but she didn't care.
There was death to be wrought. Life to be butchered.

She gazed at Zroya with empty elation and took a step
toward him at the exact moment the rapturous singing started
again.

Torin Torin Torin here here here Torin Torin Torin.

A warm light rolled over her. Through her. Her stomach
clenched and her sex throbbed. Numb and burning with living
fire, she turned to the altar, to the light. To Torin's still body.

White-gold radiance flooded the temple, blinding her.
Illuminating everything in stark clarity. She saw the blood
trickle past Torin's lips. Saw it drip from his chin, a perfect
crimson bead. Saw it fall to the blood-stained altar beneath
him. Saw it seep into the ancient stone. New blood to old.

And then she saw the Sword.

It appeared at Torin's limp fingers, rising hilt first from the
white-gold light. She stared at it, her throat tight, her heart
hammering. It was beautiful. Terrifying. It radiated infinite
power and humble force. It called her. It petrified her. She
stared at it, watching it rise from the light, every molecule of her
body burning.

Here here here here.

It continued to rise from the light, untouched by any hand,
its golden, burning length skimming past Torin's knuckles, his
wrist, in a gentle caress Kala felt on her own flesh.

Here here here here.

"Here," Uloch screeched behind her. "It is here. The
Immortals' blade. The Sun Sword. It is here."

"At last," Zroya hissed.

"Take it, Kala Rei," Uloch yelled, his voice high and

commanding. "Take it in your hand and release it of its prison."

"*What?*" Zroya's stunned shout slammed into Kala. "*I* am the One Who Burns, not her!" He stared at Uloch, furious disbelief twisting his handsome face. "*I* am the One who will control all the worlds. You said it was me. *Me*. You said *I* was the One Who—"

"Take the sword, Kala Rei," Uloch ordered over Zroya's roars, his exultant stare fixed on her. "*You* are the One Who Burns. The Oracle saw you. My brother saw you. But only *I* saw a millennium ago what you really are, what you really can be. *You* are the One Who Burns and *all* the worlds will tremble at your feet." He stepped closer to her, spittle glistening on his lips, the veins in his neck and temples bulging. "Take the sword and destroy the male who raped you. Take the sword and destroy the man for all the women he has violated and butchered. Take the sword and destroy him for all the men who have violated you. Free it from its prison and pare him in two." His voice rose higher, higher, his white eyes as bright as the golden heat filling the temple. "Show him the wrath of the Sun Sword's truth. Show him the power of the One Who Burns. Offer his death as a sacrifice to the Sword and I will show you how to use that power to make *all* the worlds burn. *All* the worlds suffer for your pain."

Kala stared at him, her blood on fire, the singing in her head frenzied. Myriad memories smashed through her—a lifetime of hideous, agonizing memories Uloch had released from the depths of her tormented soul. The pain of each one tore through her, scorching. Scalding.

Here here here here.

She ground her teeth, fighting the nightmare of those memories. "I never wanted power," she growled, burning alive from the inside out. "I only wanted Torin."

Uloch's eyes flashed silver rage. "*Take the Sword.*"

"No!" Zroya screeched again. He leapt for her, hate and fury and insane hunger in his eyes. "It is mine! Mine! You will not—"

He froze. As if every muscle suddenly turned to ice.

Uloch stepped closer to Kala again, destroying the distance between them. "Kill him," he ordered in a harsh snarl, his face twisted with contempt. "For every male that attacked you in your life, for every man who chained you, beat you. For every man who brutalized your flesh with his lust. Take the sword and cleave him in two."

Images blasted at Kala, potent, fresh memories ripe with smoldering rage. She saw Zroya loom over her, smirking down at her as he pinned her to the floor. Felt his hands rip at her flesh, her breasts, her thighs. Tasted her own blood weep into her mouth from her lips split by his fists, punctured by his teeth. Tasted his spit on her tongue from his savage kisses. She lived his assault all over again in the space of a heartbeat.

She saw him doing the very same to woman after woman, girl after girl, child after child. All in the pursuit of the One Who Burns and the Sun Sword.

The Sun Sword will bring brutal death...

In the hands of the False Fire.

She sucked in an icy breath, another, another. Her palms itched and her sex throbbed. A blistering cold, hungry heat licked at her core. Her soul. She wanted to take the sword. She *wanted* to take it and butcher Zroya where he stood. She *wanted* to plunge its burning length into his black, malicious heart and watch his blood flow from his body. She was *meant* to do this. She was *created* to do this.

...bring brutal death...

To bring brutal death to the man who had violated her. To

the man who had taken from her what was not his to take. *His* brutal death was just the beginning. A blood sacrifice. A righteous punishment. Zroya's brutal death would begin it all. The beginning of the end for the worlds of man. And her empty fury would rage forever.

No.

A calm voice whispered through her head.

Kala's breath caught. The heat in her soul flickered as if a gentle breeze blew across its raging flames.

Her eyebrows pulled into a puzzled frown. *Torin?*

"Kill him!" Uloch's cry tore the chilly air. "And open yourself to the unending power of the Immortals' weapon."

"Remember the Sun Sword's truth," the calm voice continued. Torin's voice. From a training session a lifetime ago.

"In the hands of the One Who Burns the Sun Sword will bring new life to the hearts of man. In the hands of the False Fire the Sun Sword will bring brutal death."

An incredulous disbelief stole over Kala. She froze, every fibre in her body prickling with hesitant realization.

Was she both?

No, that couldn't be. She was insane. She was—

The Youngest's seed will be perverted and the perversion will hold the hearts of man in empty fury.

The single line from the *Sol* Prophecy slipped through her head and she gasped.

Empty fury.

Her empty fury.

God, was she both? The savior *and* the destroyer? The seed and the perversion? The One Who Burns *and* the False Fire?

The prickling sensation intensified and she sucked in a

sharp breath. If she took the sword now, who would draw Zroya's blood?

God, had Torin known all along?

Uloch stared at her, his eyes blazing a silver inferno of malevolent fury. "Kill him, Kala Rei, and I will lead you to glory and dominion over all."

She shook her head, her heart racing. "No."

"Kill him."

"No."

"Kill him!"

"No."

Icy contempt warped Uloch's triumphant expression to a twisted sneer. "Very well then," he snarled. "I shall do it for you."

He curled his right hand around the dead rabbit's rotting head, tightened his grip on its hind legs with his left and ripped the carcass apart.

"Master?" Confusion and terror turned Zroya's squeal to a strangled squeak. "What is—" His eyes rolled, his mouth stretched wide and—with a sickening, wet *glurk*—his body tore in two.

Blood sprayed over Uloch. He laughed, the viscous liquid spattering his face in grotesque patterns, his white eyes blazing brighter. "Now, Kala Rei!" His jubilant cry reverberated throughout the temple, throughout Kala's stomach. "Take the sword."

"The Sun Sword will bring new life to the hearts of man in the hands of the One Who Burns..." The words of the prophecy whispered in her head, her soul.

Golden heat reached out for her.

"The Sun Sword will bring brutal death to the hearts of man

in the hands of the False Fire."

"The One Who Burns restores life where there is death. Brings death where there is life."

Her pulse quickened.

"Pierce the undead heart with the burning heart..."

Her breath grew shallow.

"Pierce the undead heart with the burning heart..."

"Take the sword, Kala Rei. Take it! Take it!"

Take the sword, Kala.

The last command whispered through Kala's mind. Soft. Calm. Trusting. Her own voice. No one else's.

Uloch stepped closer, impatient fury devouring his blood-streaked face. "Take the sword, Kala Rei and fulfill my vision!"

Kala narrowed her eyes in a disgusted glare. "Go to hell, old man. And take a bath while you're there." She curled her lip and wrinkled her nose. "You stink."

She spun to the altar, her blood roaring in her ears, her heart thumping in her throat. Just as the Sun Sword burst into golden fire.

The white light radiating from its blade grew blindingly hot, bathing Torin's lifeless body in a pure glow of heat, concealing him, shrouding him. She extended her arm, her blood molten lava, her heart a steady tattoo, and curled her fingers around the hilt of the sword.

Here here here now now now.

Now.

She ignited. Fire. White-hot. Incinerating.

Completing.

Pierce the undead heart with the burning heart...

Calm descended over her. Her heartbeat slowed. Her breath

grew steady. She knew what she was doing. As well as she knew Torin loved her. For what she was—an abused girl he'd found on a dying planet with anger and hate in her soul. For what she had become—the One Who Burns.

The One Who Burns restores life where there is death.

The One Who Burns brings death where there is life.

She raised the Sun Sword above her shoulder with graceful strength, swung its perfect weight in a smooth arc above her head, leveled her unwavering stare on her target—*"No!"* Uloch screamed—and plunged the burning blade into Torin's lifeless chest.

Done.

The word sounded in Kala's head, a pure crystal voice of infinite time and power, and the Sun Sword detonated into white energy, white life, white heat and incinerated everything.

Everything.

Torin opened his eyes. There was no pain, no heat, just light. White light. He drew in a slow breath, letting it pour into his being.

A serene calm came with its cool caress, flowing through him, seeking out the centre of his existence. He frowned, studying the ubiquitous whiteness. Where was he?

Pushing himself to his feet, he cocked his head to the side. Why was he here?

"To hear and to learn."

Torin turned at the familiar voice behind him, narrowing his eyes. The Old Seer stood in the light, vivid in clarity and wearing a small smile, his skin as leathered and seamed as it ever had been, his eyes as sightless and unerringly piercing as they had always been. "I did warn you she would be your undoing, Torin Kerridon."

"She?" He gave the Old Seer a reproachful look, ignoring the fact he was talking to a man long since dead. A man he himself had set torch to while laid out on a pyre in the P'helios willows. "I do think you failed to mention the gender of the One Who Burns in your guidance, Seer."

"Did I?" The ancient man's smile turned enigmatic. "Would it have made a difference?"

Torin ground his teeth. "Yes," he answered with flat conviction. "It would have."

The Old Seer studied him with those penetrating, sightless eyes and said nothing.

A heavy pressure wrapped around Torin's chest and he curled his fingers into fists. He had no idea where he was—Hell? The next life?—but he didn't care. He glared at his old guide. "You knew Uloch would take her."

The Old Seer's expression remained composed. "Yes."

"You knew she would be tortured by your brother."

"Yes."

Torin closed his eyes, cold rage cutting his calm. He'd never been angry with his *Sol* guide before. Exasperated, yes, but never angry. His rage was unnerving and powerful. He swallowed a thick lump in his throat and ground out the statement weighing most heavily on his chest. "You knew I would fall in love with her."

"Yes."

Opening his eyes, he let the old man see his rage. "You knew and yet you chose not to tell me."

The Old Seer raised his eyebrows, as if surprised by Torin's accusation. "I told you the Old Who Burns would be your undoing."

"My *undoing*?" Torin bit back a furious curse. "I don't give a flying fuck about my undoing. Do you know what Kala has suffered since I found her? If I'd known, I—"

He stopped, the lump in his throat growing thicker. If he'd know he'd what? Never gone to Earth in the first place? Never taken Kala from the hellhole of her life there? Never held her in his arms and let her have his heart? He shook his head and swallowed at the lump once more. He must be dead. Where else but the lowest pit of the next life would he be tormented so?

"You are not in the next phase of your existence, Torin Kerridon."

The Old Seer's calm voice made him tighten his fists even as a cold weight pressed on his heart. He studied his old guide, fighting against the numb acknowledgment of the situation threading into his being. "But I am undone."

"Yes, you are."

Torin growled, his patience fraying. "If I am not in the next life, old man, then where am I? Where is Kala?"

The Old Seer smiled again. Enigmatic. Calm. "You are waiting."

"Waiting?" Torin grappled with the black anger twisting through his tenuous control. "For what?"

"To allow the question and the answer."

Torin closed his eyes again and pulled a steadying breath. The white light flowed through him once more but this time there came no serenity. Syunna, was his old guide always this frustrating? Eyes still closed, he began a slow count to one hundred, focusing on each muscle in his body one at a time. Forcing calm into every individual one.

"When you allow yourself to acknowledge the question and the answer in your soul your waiting will end."

He opened his eyes and glared at the ancient man, his meditation forgotten. "I know of no question, old man. Only a statement uttered to me by someone I once thought I could trust. *'The One Who Burns will be your undoing. And your end'.*"

The Old Seer nodded, and if he was hurt by Torin's words he did not show it. "Yes."

Torin studied him, the anger in his blood growing thicker. He didn't want to be here—wherever "here" was. He wanted to be with Kala. He wanted to hold her close and take away every second of pain he'd brought to her life. He wanted to say sorry. He wanted to tell her he loved her. He wanted to spend the rest of their lives together. Curse it, if he wasn't dead, why was he—

An icy fist punched into his soul and his mouth turned dry. "She took the sword. Kala took the sword, didn't she?"

"Yes."

"Is she dead?"

The Old Seer didn't respond. Just stood there in the omnipresent white light, sightless eyes holding Torin's glare.

The icy fist slammed into him again. "Is. Kala. Dead?"

Silence.

No. No, by the gods, no.

He took a step forward, hands balled into fists. "Is Kala Rei dead, old man?"

The Old Seer shook his head. "That is not the question you seek the answer to, last command warrior of the *Sol* Order."

Torin's rage turned hot. "There is no other question more important," he snapped.

The Old Seer smiled. "There is, Torin. A most important question and answer."

181

He squeezed his fists tighter. "*What* answer? *What* question?"

The old man's eyelids fluttered closed. "In the hands of the One Who Burns, the heart of the lone will bring force to the Sun Sword, destroying the dark and giving birth to the light. In the hands of the False Fire, the Sun Sword will bring death to the heart of the lone and the light will consume all."

Torin clenched his jaw and took another step forward. "Damn you, Seer. Enough of the prophecy crap. I get it. I am a part of it as much as Kala, but I don't care! Is the woman I love alive?"

The Old Seer raised his eyebrows again. "Who is the woman you love, Torin Kerridon? Have you pondered that? The One Who Burns? The ultimate warrior? A woman powered by peace and acceptance? " He held his head at an angle, a quizzical expression on his seamed face. "Or the False Fire? The ultimate weapon? A woman fueled by hate and revenge? Who *is* Kala Rei? " He paused, his white eyes revealing nothing. "To you?"

Torin lifted his chin and fixed the man who had guided him since birth with a level, defiant stare. "She is both."

"So tell me, Torin," the old man went on, as calm and composed as always, "which one took the blade? The woman loved by you, or the woman tortured by every other living soul she has ever known?" His sightless stare grew intent, his expression more ambiguous than ever. "Who woke the sword forged by the Eldest Immortal from its slumber, poured heat into its existence and plunged it into your heart? The seed? Or the perversion?"

Torin met his *Sol* guide's unseeing gaze, his chest tight, his blood a surging pressure through his veins. He'd trained Kala to wield the ultimate weapon, but in doing so had he made her the very weapon he'd dedicated his life protecting the worlds of man against? He loved her more than he thought ever possible, but was it enough to heal her heart?

You gave your word.

And still you made me scream.

Kala's words from his nightmare sliced into him. He squeezed his eyes closed, pressed his face into his hands. His guilt rolled through him like sludge. He'd promised her he would never...

The sludge oozed through his soul, lapped at his heart.

He'd made her scream. He'd broken his word. He'd hurt her when he promised he wouldn't. He'd taken her when he swore he would not. He'd loved her when...

A steady beat thumped in his throat and Kala's words came back to him, *"For everything you have let me become, Torin Kerridon, I love you. For everything I am since you saved me, I love you."*

Realization flowed through him like a silken wave and he smiled. He understood it now. There was no need for contemplation or hesitation. No need for consideration or anxious worriment. There was no need for waiting. He knew the answer. His heart knew the answer as surely as his soul knew the question. Lifting his face from his hands, he opened his eyes and looked at the old man standing before him. "The One Who Burns plunged the blade into my heart, Old Seer," he said with more conviction than any words he'd ever uttered before. "And she burns for me."

The ancient seer smiled, his expression calmly happy. "Yes, my child." He dipped his head in a single nod. "She does."

And then the white light enveloped him in a blinding, consuming eruption, and Torin stood alone in its pure, cleansing brilliance.

✧

"Torin?"

Torin opened his eyes. There was no pain, no heat, just light. White light. And Kala. Standing over him.

He smiled, levering himself up onto his elbows. "The One Who Burns shall be your undoing," he murmured.

Kala stood motionless, her stare locked on his face, her expression guarded. Hesitant. She looked like she wanted to move, but she held still, her hands empty, her lips parted. "You're...you're..." An exasperated frown suddenly pulled at her eyebrows and she shook her head, shoving her hands on her hips. "What the hell does *that* mean?"

"Yes, I am alive," he said with a grin, finishing what he knew she stuttered over. "And it is something the Old Seer told me a lifetime ago." He gave a low, wry chuckle. "Something tells me now it doesn't mean what he—what *we*—thought it did."

Kala's expression grew more guarded, but hope shone in her eyes. "What do you think it means now, Torin?"

He let his smile fade as he rose to his feet, towering over her as he always did. "It means you tore me apart, Kala." He took a step closer to her, her heat on his body a caress he never wanted to be without, an undeniable force that gave him strength beyond comprehension. He gazed down into her face. "Everything I was, everything I knew, you tore apart. Rendering me unmade, vulnerable and defenseless."

She studied him for a long moment, so still she didn't appear to breathe. "I didn't mean to undo you, *Sol* warrior," she finally said, her voice solemn and grave. And then she grinned and the hope in her eyes sparkled with cheeky mischief. "But I'm glad I did."

184

Torin chuckled, skimming his gaze over the empty temple around them. His heart skipped a beat when he saw the carved image of himself standing above the altar, heart and sword in hand, an image chiseled into the stone over half a millennium ago, and then he returned his attention to the only thing that mattered. "So—" he smiled down into Kala's face, "—you've finally accepted who you are."

She gave him a small shrug. "It seems so."

He let his stare wander her face, the pit of his belly growing tight. She'd always been beautiful—stubborn, yes, surly, at times—but now she seemed to glow. Now, she seemed...to burn.

He pulled a slow breath, dragging his gaze from her eyes to scan the temple again. "Where is Uloch? And the walking corpse?"

"Uloch...Uloch tore Zroya in two and..." She stopped and he looked at her again, watching an uncomfortable expression flicker over her face.

"And when you plunged the Sun Sword into my heart?" he offered, giving her a small grin.

"And when I plunged the sword into your heart, Uloch turned to..."

"Toast?"

Kala rolled her eyes, scowling at him. "You know, I think I like you better when you're a bastard beating the crap out of me in the training room."

Torin chuckled. "There are other things we can do in the training room, Kala Rei."

She rolled her eyes again, shaking her head, but she didn't move. The corners of her lips twitched. "You've just been resurrected from the dead by a weapon made by immortal beings from existence's very heart, a weapon that vanished the second it pierced *your* heart, a weapon that doesn't seem to exist anymore and all you can think about it sex?"

"You're wrong, Kala." He shook his head, taking the one step left between them, sliding his hands over her hips to tug her close to his body. "The Sun Sword will always exist, even when it can not be seen." He lowered his head, brushing his lips against her cheek. "And all I can think about is you. The One Who Burns, the False Fire, the tiny slip of a thing covered in filth I found on Earth who beat me to the ground with nothing but her courage and a steel pipe."

Kala studied him, a frown pulling at her dark eyebrows. "So, you *did* know all along. The One Who Burns and the False Fire *are* one and the same." Her frown deepened. "And yet you still trained me. You still told me about the power of the sword and what it was capable of." She paused, the expression on her face more than puzzled. "Why? How could you know what I'd do? Which one I'd become in the moment of truth?"

Torin placed a soft kiss on the tip of her nose. "I didn't."

Kala's eyes widened and she pulled away from him a little. "But the prophecy? The worlds of man? Death, destruction? I could have destroyed it all. I could feel the power of the Sun Sword in me. It was terrifying and seductive all at once. If I'd wanted to, I could have extinguished every star in every universe with just a single thought. If I'd wanted to, I could have placed a fire in every living soul and let them burn alive. And I almost did. I came so close..." She pulled farther from his body, disbelief shining in her eyes. "How could you risk that? How could you—"

"You need to listen to me, Kala Rei." He chuckled, tugging her back into his embrace and smoothing his hand up her back. "I believe in *you*. Not the One Who Burns, not the False Fire. You. I have since the second you threatened to castrate me

186

back on Earth." He placed his lips on her forehead. "And it seems the Sun Sword believes in you too." He smiled. "Being that I'm alive and all." He folded his arms around her waist and held her close, breathing in her scent before kissing her gently on the lips. "Thank you for that."

She looked up at him, the corners of her mouth curling, her green eyes sparkling gold heat. "You're welcome," she murmured, tugging his head down to hers. "You're very, very welcome."

She kissed him back with a little more force, a little more heat. Her lips parted under his, her tongue slipping into his mouth, her hands stealing up his back to tangle in his hair. Holding him to her with undeniable love and desire.

Setting him on fire.

Making him burn.

And burn.

Epilogue

Kala Rei stepped out of the lost *Sol* temple, stretching her arms above her head. She lifted her face to the night sky, pulling in a slow breath as she studied the stars' glinting beauty. They were completely foreign to her but she knew them all the same and, as she gazed at their strange constellations, a warm sense of comfort rolled over her.

She smiled as the words of the prophecy she'd fought so hard to deny came to her. *In the hands of the One Who Burns the Sun Sword will bring new life to the hearts of man.*

Kala smoothed her hands up and down her arms, smiling wider. Not the "hearts of man". Just one man. One very important man. What happened to the rest of the known universes now, she and that one man would discover together.

Hugging herself against the cool air, she let her thoughts turn to the Immortals' weapon. The Sun Sword smoldered in gentle slumber within her existence, a simmering heat radiating through her from its new home within her soul. She didn't understand how she knew it was there, nor in fact, how it could be, but she did. It wasn't just that she could "feel" its presence. It was more than that. It was symbiotic. Its warmth charged her with life and her life charged it with heat. If she needed to, if the worlds of man needed her to, she would draw the sword again from its mystical sheath and do what she was created to do—

bring death where there was life and life where there was death. For now however, all she wanted to do was return to Torin's arms and make love to him.

She let out a contented sigh, letting her gaze move among the stars without really seeing them.

"Do they call you, Kala?" Large, strong hands slipped around her waist, tugging her back against a body just as large, just as strong, and she closed her eyes with a smile. Torin pressed his face to the side of her neck, his lips nuzzling the sensitive dip below her ear. "Do the stars ask you to come to them? To set them on fire?"

She leant into his body, rolling her head to the side to grant his mouth delicious access to her neck. She loved the way he kissed her there, with a tenderness so reverent it stole her breath and made her knees weak.

"They do." She ran her hands up Torin's arms, to his shoulders, turning in his embrace as she did so to gaze up into his eyes. "But they can wait."

He cocked an eyebrow, slipping his hands down her hips to rest lightly on her backside. "Really? And what pressing business does the One Who Burns have that the worlds of man must wait for her fire?"

She rose up onto her toes and rolled her hips, stroking the curve of her sex against the growing length of his erection trapped behind the taut leather of his trousers. "I have a fire here that needs tending."

Torin's eyes glinted in the pale moonlight and he tightened his grip on her arse, pulling her hips harder to his. "This fire will never be smothered, Kala. Will never be extinguished." He lowered his head and placed a gentle kiss on her lips. "This is something you should know."

She chuckled, tangling her fingers in the shaggy length of

his hair. "Are you trying to scare me off, *Sol*?"

His nostrils flared and he squeezed her arse, pulling her closer still to his rigid cock. "Does this feel like I'm trying to scare you off?"

Before she could answer, he yanked her feet off the ground and wrapped her legs around his hips, turning on the spot to press her back to the carved rock wall of the temple's entrance. She gasped, delight rippling through her in a hot wave as, without a word, he grabbed the bunched hem of the cotton slave shift she still wore and tore it over her head.

The cool night air of the P'Helios moon caressed her naked body, turned her nipples into rock-hard points. She sucked in a swift breath, her breath becoming a whimpered moan when Torin closed his hands over her breasts and captured her nipples between his knuckles.

"Does this feel like I am trying to frighten you away?" he murmured, pinching the puckered tips of flesh with an urgency Kala could feel all the way to her core. His shoulder muscles bunched, his stomach muscles flexed, and before Kala knew what he was doing, he'd pressed her harder to the stone wall. "Or does this feel like I am ready to burn with you hotter than before?"

He slid partly down her body, supporting her weight with his broad chest, one hand flat to the base of her spine, the other still cupping her breast. He tweaked her nipple with his knuckles one more time, sending jolts of liquid heat through her, and then closed his lips around its distended shape and drew it into his mouth.

Kala moaned, gripping her legs tighter around his torso, the pulling suction on her breast flooding her sex with warm moisture. She fisted her hands in his hair and gazed up at the stars, her lips parting as her breath grew shallow.

No, this did not feel like he was trying to scare her off. Not at all.

He bit her nipple with gentle force, once, twice, and she moaned again, her head swimming with dizzy pleasure, her heart thumping with building rapture. This felt like he was trying to set her on fire.

And she was more than ready to be engulfed by the flames.

More than ready to be incinerated by his heat.

She was, after all, the One Who Burns.

About the Author

Lexxie's not a deviant. She just has a deviant's imagination and a desire to entertain readers with her words. Add the two together and you get darkly erotic romances with a twist of horror, sci-fi and the paranormal.

When she's not submerged in the worlds she creates, Lexxie's life revolves around her family, a husband who thinks she's insane, a pony-sized mutt who thinks he's a lapdog, two yabbies hell-bent on destroying their tank and her daughters, who both utterly captured her heart and changed her life forever.

Contact Lexxie at Lexxie@lexxiecouper.com, follow her on Twitter http://twitter.com/lexxie_couper or visit her at www.lexxiecouper.com where she occasionally makes a fool of herself on her blog.

Is he the hero of her childhood dreams...
or the death of them—and her?

Prophesied
© *2008 Liz Craven*

On the day of her birth, Lia fulfilled a prophecy that ended a 5,000-year war, and became a wife. But being the fulfillment of a sacred prophecy makes for a stifling childhood—not to mention a dangerous one. When an assassination attempt goes wrong, Lia takes the opportunity and runs from her destiny—as well as from her absent husband.

Talon isn't sure what to expect when he rescues his bride from a mining colony on a barren moon. What he doesn't anticipate is her lack of gratitude and her repeated escape attempts. Determined to convince his wife to accept her duties, Talon knows he also needs to keep her safe, even if he has to lock her up in his own quarters to do it.

As they get closer to their planet and Lia's coronation, the danger around them increases, and so does the tension between them. For their growing attraction to turn into something more, they need to stay alive and learn to trust each other—a tall order when Lia's experience in life has taught her that trusting people can get you killed.

Warning: Contains adult language, sexual content, and as always, reading anything by Liz Craven may be hazardous to your sanity.

Available now in ebook and print from Samhain Publishing.

Enjoy the following excerpt from Prophesied...

Lia's eyes, accustomed to the dark mines, burned under the harsh office light. Blinking the tears back, the face of the speaking soldier wavered briefly, before coming into focus.

Her heart stuttered, and she managed to keep her jaw from dropping. Just when she thought things couldn't get any worse—or any better, she wasn't sure which.

His face was leaner than she remembered, giving his cheekbones a sharp edge. He had lost the soft features of a young man. The roundness of his cheeks had faded, making his square jaw more pronounced and giving him a determined look. He regarded the rep with gray eyes, the color of melted xyreon ore when light struck it. Unlike the ore, however, his flinty eyes were ice cold. The world "ruthless" flitted across her mind and a shiver danced down her spine.

His body had been long and lanky when she had last seen him, but the man before her was not the awkward boy she once knew. His chest had filled out, making him easily three times her width. His upper torso tapered to a lean waist. Body armor hugged trim hips and strong legs. The red emblem of an elected planetary official gleamed on his shoulders.

He barely glanced at her, and the feeling of disappointment that swept over Lia surprised her. She hadn't wanted him to recognize her and had no business feeling hurt because she had gotten her wish.

As she studied him, he glanced at a soldier behind him and jerked his chin in her direction. A man with blond hair and the flush of youth still in his cheeks stepped towards her. He smiled at her—the first courtesy ever offered to her in the rep's office—and extended his arm.

"This will only take a moment," the young soldier assured her.

Staring at the device he was holding, Lia took a cautious step back. The rep still had a death grip on her arm—her fingers were going numb—so the step was small, but it was enough for the soldier to hesitate.

"What is that?" she demanded, relieved she sounded angry rather than panicked.

"It won't hurt." His tone was polite, if condescending, but he didn't lower the device.

"What 'won't hurt'?" Lia snapped out.

The young man actually blushed. "It's a simple DNA scan. It will take less than five seconds, and you won't feel a thing."

This time Lia wrenched her arm free from the rep as she leaped backwards. "Absolutely not."

"I promise it won't hurt," the youth reassured her.

"I said no."

Then *he* spoke, and he had the audacity to sound amused. "Madam, we are looking for someone. The DNA scan will help narrow our search by eliminating you. We will compensate you for your time."

She snorted. Even if they gave her money, the rep would be the one "compensated" for her time. "I still refuse."

"We must insist."

Ignoring the furious glare of the rep, she stood her ground. "Under League privacy laws, a DNA scan cannot be compelled unless an individual is under arrest. Am I under arrest?"

He lifted an eyebrow. She resisted the urge to reach up and yank it back down.

"You are not under arrest—" he conceded.

"Then I am free to refuse the scan."

"Neither are you in League territory," he continued. He gestured towards the youth. "Caden."

Lia's stomach sank. They had her. League laws meant nothing on Tmesis. The only thing she could do was endure the scan with dignity.

The young soldier stepped forward, pointing the scanner at her.

Dignity be damned. With fury fueled by fear, Lia kicked out, knocking the scanner from the unsuspecting soldier's hand. She spun and darted for the door.

She didn't make it three meters, before slamming into another one of the soldiers who had circled around to block her path with inhuman speed. Her breathing hitched when she took in his glowing red eyes, wide-spread jaw, and sharp pointed teeth. An Inderian. A proud and fierce race of warriors steeped in tradition, blood feuds, and honor. If their inherent skills weren't enough to inspire fear in those they met, the rumors of ritual sacrifice and cannibalism were. They rarely left their home system, but those who did usually hired out as assassins.

Were the soldiers seeking her out to ensure her death?

The Inderian turned Lia to face the others, lifting her completely off her feet to do so, and she hated that her face was flushed. The impromptu flight embarrassed her. Where did she think she was going? There weren't a lot of hiding places on a barren moon. Especially when you needed pesky little luxuries like water. Fortunately, the dirt and grime smearing her face hid her blush. At least she hoped they did.

He stood in the same place, his arms crossed and that infuriating eyebrow still cocked, making no effort to hide his amusement.

Caden held the scanner again, his gaze flicking back and

forth between Lia and his commander who met Lia's narrowed eyes for a brief moment before nodding.

Caden approached her cautiously, like drawing near a nest of vipers. Lia felt a crazy urge to laugh. The Inderian held her immobilized. She could barely turn her head, much less attack a trained soldier. She wasn't fooling herself. The only reason she'd succeeded in kicking him before was the element of surprise.

No miner in their right mind would attack a League soldier. Lia supposed that meant she was no longer in her right mind. Not that it mattered, seeing how they were probably going to kill her.

She had feared for her life for as long as she could remember and had half-expected to feel relief at finally facing death. She didn't. She was pissed-off, plain and simple. And under the anger, her heart ached that the one good thing she remembered from childhood—this cold and *amused* man—was an illusion.

An illusion that was probably going to kill her.

Caden pressed a button and a beam of orange light moved over her. The crucial procedure took mere seconds. The light disappeared, and Caden began inputting data into the scanner.

Scrapping together what little dignity she had left, Lia addressed the Inderian. "You can release me now."

A nod from their leader, and she found herself standing on her own two feet. The Inderian shifted behind her and she knew he prepared to catch her if she bolted. He needn't have bothered. With the scan completed, she felt oddly resigned and drained of energy. With her anger gone, the long day, the cave-in and her injury finally caught up with her. Not to mention the strain of the last five minutes. She wanted to sit down. Actually, she wanted to curl into fetal position. She did neither.

A pair of boots stepped into her field of vision and she looked up into the face of the man from her past.

"That wasn't so bad, was it?" The brisk tone lacked warmth, but Lia sensed he was trying to be kind. Her anger had amused him. She wondered if her dejection bothered him.

She decided to answer his question honestly. "Yes, it was."

He blinked, and she realized she had surprised him. Instinctively, she knew very little surprised this man.

He inclined his head politely. "I apologize for the inconvenience." He hesitated before dropping his voice to prevent the rep from overhearing. "We only seek to find a missing person. The scan will be used to eliminate your DNA as a match for hers. Once done, you will be free to go. We will not be passing scan results on to authorities or storing them in any public database. Your privacy and secrets will remain intact."

He thought her a criminal afraid of being caught. She was about to surprise him again.

He turned away from her, dismissing her. "Caden, I believe we have taken up enough of this young lady's time. Record her as a non-match and reset the scanner for the next subject."

"I can't," Caden sounded nervous.

"You can't? The scanner is malfunctioning?"

"No, sir. I just ran and reran a diagnostic on it. I also ran the results four times," Caden rushed to assure him.

"Then what seems to be the problem?"

"There's no problem. It's just that..." He hesitated.

"That what?" the commander barked.

"I'm a match," Lia said wearily. "I'm your wife.

GREAT
cheap
fun

Discover eBooks!

THE FASTEST WAY TO GET THE HOTTEST NAMES

Get your favorite authors on your favorite reader, long before they're
out in print! Ebooks from Samhain go wherever you go, and work with
whatever you carry—Palm, PDF, Mobi, and more.

Samhain
publishing
LTD

WWW.SAMHAINPUBLISHING.COM

CPSIA information can be obtained at www.ICGtesting.com
Printed in the USA
BVOW072233040713

325107BV00001B/58/P

9 781605 048222